Dead Boy Talking

Linda Strachan

Published by
Strident Publishing Ltd
22 Strathwhillan Drive
The Orchard, Hairmyres
East Kilbride G75 8GT

Tel: +44 (0)1355 220588
info@stridentpublishing.co.uk
www.stridentpublishing.co.uk

YA

A catalogue record for this book is
available from the British Library.

ISBN 978-1-905537-20-4

Typeset in Warnock Pro
Designed by Sallie Moffat

The publisher acknowledges subsidy
from the Scottish Arts Council.

Dedication

This book is dedicated to Euan Tippen and Tommy Smail, for their valuable comments on an early draft of the book.

Acknowledgments

I would like to thank some very special young people from North Berwick High school's
Platinum Pages Publication Promotions,
namely—Neil Wilson, Jessica Tate, Finlay Patrick, Peter Mortimer, Margaret McPake, Christopher McHardy, Finlay MacDonald, Ellie McArthur, Chloe Kandirikirira, Calum Jenkins, Pornthewa Horthong, Emma Hay, Rhianna Hardie, Finlay Hall, David Fletcher, Andrew Duncan, Liberty Davidson, Michael Cleary, Callum Burns and Sarah Adam—for their enthusiasm, imagination and enterprise in taking on the idea for a project based on this book, and making it their own.

Special thanks also to Susan Conway, their teacher, and to Superintendent John Hawkins of Lothian and Borders Police.

My thanks to the wonderful team at Strident: Keith, Alison, Graham and Sallie who are always a pleasure to work with, my agent Kathryn and as always my family, for their support and encouragement.

Linda Strachan is the author of over 50 books for all ages. Her first novel for teenagers, the highly acclaimed *Spider*, was nominated for several literary awards. Before becoming a full-time writer she was a model, a medical lab technician and a fashion buyer. She likes dogs, painting pictures on walls, artichokes, olives and chocolate, but prefers writing to almost anything else.

Contents

In 25 minutes I will be dead.

The knife slipped into my body, a bright, sharp edge of death, a thief. It sliced easily through leather, skin and flesh. Hot, red blood coating its blade, warming the icy metal with a precious, searing heat. It flowed over the handle and escaped, rushing in a fiery torrent, taking my life with it.

No, this is not some dead person talking from the grave. It's just me, Josh, you know me.

I'm not scared.

I'm not!

Yeah, who am I kidding?

It can't really be happening to me, can it?

They say it takes about 25 minutes to bleed to death. I want to scream and yell but there's no one here to hear me and I...I can't breathe enough to yell anyway.

I'm going to die here, all on my own.

Help me...someone, please, come and help me!

1

I hardly feel anything at first; thinking he'd missed me I'm about to laugh about it with Danny when I see his face in the fading light. He's staring at my jacket.

'What?' I bark at him.

He opens his mouth and shuts it again without making a sound, looking like an actor in a silent movie.

'What?'

My first thought is that he'd cut my jacket. I'm real proud of my new jacket. I look down and see the gaping edges of the leather flapping open, it's ruined. Danny's staring 'cos he knows how much the jacket means to me.

No! Part of me knows that's not it, but my thoughts are chasing around my head crashing into each other and making no sense, refusing to believe.

I start to laugh but my breath vanishes in an icy purple stripe of pain. I grab at the pain to make it stop and stare in disbelief at my hand, a thick, sticky, glove of blood.

All that hot, red blood pouring out, all over me.

He's done more than cut my jacket. That's why Danny is still staring at me like that.

It can't be...that means...Nooooo!

I want to puke. My head is spinning, and my legs are shaking so much that I can't stand. I lean against the wall and slide to the ground.

That's better. I can begin to breathe again. Each breath hurts, so I taste the air in little sips.

It's late and the clouds are creeping in quickly, cloaking ground and trees in shadows, turning them grey and lifeless, but it's me that will be lifeless and grey. Death is lurking, waiting in the shadows.

Was it only yesterday morning when everything started to go wrong? Then it was me, standing over Ranj's bleeding body, my knife covered in his blood. I never imagined that could happen. I only carried the knife because it was Gary's and just in case I got into trouble from the likes of Harry, but I never really thought I'd use it—then everything happened so quickly.

Is this what Ranj felt like? Hurting...scared...confused?

Oh God, NO! I'm going to DIE!

ONE: The Day Before – The Alley

Sunday morning

The bloodied blade rolled down his nerveless fingers, sticking for a moment before it fell and clattered against the concrete, blood splattering, knife spinning to the ground. The winter sun was low that morning. It glared off the grey-white scribed walls of the alleyway making them look bright and sharp so that the blood droplets shone like red jewels against the graffiti.

'Run!' shrieked Danny. 'For God's sake, Josh, we've got to get out of here!'

Josh stared at Ranj. He could hear every tiny sound like they had been amplified in his head; the whistle in Danny's chest as air forced its way in and out of his mouth in rapid gasps, the distant sound of traffic on the Hale Road; the wind pushing dried leaves along the path, rustling and whispering. Worst of all was that strange kind of moan coming from Ranj as he lay bleeding out onto the ground.

Forcing himself to concentrate Josh realised he had to try to get his head straight, and quickly. He and Danny were the only ones still there. Sensing disaster Harry's gang, the YHT, had evaporated into the air as if they had not just been crowding around the body that lay crumpled like nothing more than a pile of clothes, bleeding, dying.

Josh couldn't think about it being a person—being Ranj.

His life was melting before his eyes and reshaping into a dark, murky gloom, out of control; a life filled with fear and secrets. He turned away unable to look at the familiar face screwed up in pain. Unwanted memories of childhood games danced past Josh's eyes, visions of a familiar wide, quirky grin dissolved into the screwed up face on the ground.

'Ranj! Can you hear me, Ranj?'

He didn't know what to do. Crouching down he tried to lift Ranj up; there was a soft scream of pain as if Ranj had almost no breath left to scream with. Josh shuddered. It was a horrible sound.

'Ranj. Speak to me!' With a groan, Ranj's eyes rolled back in his head and he slumped a dead weight in Josh's arms. 'Ranj! Omigod! Wake up, Ranj.' He shook him but Ranj didn't move at all.

'Josh, we've got to get out of here!'

Josh let Ranj's body fall back onto the ground, his hands shaking. He stared at them, smeared with warm, thick blood.

'He's dead.' The words fell from his mouth as if they were a sentence—a life sentence.

MURDERER

Bile rose in his throat. He'd used the knife, Gary's knife, and it was all a stupid mistake but a final deadly, irreversible one. Why did it have to be Ranj?

'Josh, pick up the knife!' Danny squealed at him, his voice pitched high with panic. 'We can't let them find it here.'

Josh picked up the gory, dripping knife between two fingers. It had changed, evolved as if it had taken a life of its own, once a cherished possession, now it revolted him. He didn't want to look at it, but with some part of him that was thinking more clearly he realised that he had to get rid of it properly, somewhere no one would ever find it.

Danny was right—he couldn't let anyone find it here beside Ranj, covered in Ranj's blood.

RANJ!

Pushing his thoughts away, folding them back into a dark corner of his head, he wiped the knife against the weeds growing at the foot of the wall and tucked it back into its usual place in his back pocket. Catching sight of his hands Josh stared at them, almost surprised to see that they were still covered in blood, as if he had perhaps imagined it all. He frantically wiped them against his jeans as he got up and ran off down the lane after Danny. He looked back, wanting to believe it had all been a mistake, but Ranj was still there lying slumped on the ground, dead.

Josh ran as fast as he could, quickly overtaking Danny, as if by running harder and faster he could leave it all behind him.

He ducked down Lovers Lane with the sound of Danny's heavy feet thundering close behind. They pushed past a couple too engrossed in each other to notice, out into the street and past the school railings.

Glancing behind him Josh strained to hear anything above the sound of his own laboured breathing; listening for the cries and yells that would mean Ranj had been found or the sirens that would tell him that the police had arrived.

Part of him wanted them to come quickly and find Ranj, so that he wouldn't be left lying there alone in the dirt; the other part desperately hoped that he and Danny would have time to get away. He knew, somewhere deep inside, that he shouldn't be running away, leaving Ranj lying there alone. But it was as if his feet made the decision for him, taking him further away from Ranj with every step. It was too big, too much for him to think about, so he just ran and kept on running.

Danny was gasping for breath and Josh knew he wouldn't be able to keep up this pace for long. They needed to get lost, to find somewhere they could disappear into a crowd and become anonymous. He knew just the place and leaping over a low wall, headed straight for the centre of town. Danny tried to say something but he could hardly find enough breath to run.

'Don't try to talk, Danny, just keep up,' Josh barked over his shoulder.

There was a carnival on in the town park and that meant a large crowd which would make it easy for them to get lost, even though he was fairly sure Harry and the YHT would be there too, waiting for them.

Josh ran through the streets, his brain in overdrive trying to replay the last few minutes. It all came back to him in sickening waves but he refused to let himself think about it and kept trying to focus on finding somewhere he and Danny could hide. A loud drum roll echoed from the direction of the park, the carnival parade was starting. Josh hoped everyone would be watching the parade, but just in case anyone noticed them arriving he led Danny away from the main gates to the park; it was too open there. He knew a better way in.

A gap in the fence ahead of them led on towards the park, it would take them closer to where the crowds were gathered. Checking to see that Danny was still keeping up, he jumped over a low gate to cut the corner through one of the gardens. He winced as a dog started barking inside the house. Danny laboured up behind him until he could grab the other boy's jacket, propelling him faster through the garden, over the flowerbeds.

He pushed Danny ahead of him over the low fence at the far side, with a quick look to make sure no one was coming out to investigate. Another three loud drum rolls and he could hear the cheers as the parade set off.

Normally Josh loved the carnival: the noise, the

smell, the colours and the sideshows. He and Ranj used to come every year when they were younger. He tried to push thoughts of Ranj out of his head but the image of him lying there in the alley with that fixed grimace on his face just kept creeping back in.

As they approached the gap in the park hedges Josh could see the crowds. He scanned the area looking for any familiar figures and slowed up, stopping Danny from rushing past him with an outstretched arm. It would be just plain silly to run headlong into the YHT now.

'We'll attract less attention if we walk,' he told Danny, who was leaning hands on his knees trying to catch his breath. 'Get up! Everyone will know you've been running if you stand like that!'

Still gasping for breath and red in the face, Danny did what Josh told him. He always did, it was the natural order of things.

Josh said—Danny did. That was how it was, always.

Josh knew that Danny expected him to know what to do. He seemed to think Josh was always right and sure of himself, that whatever happened Josh would always know what to do or what to say. Even now he just waited for him to take charge as usual. Danny shuddered and Josh wondered if the scene in the lane was replaying in his head, too, in sharp, harsh images.

They walked slowly, crossing the park just as the

band struck up a loud tune. Scanning the crowd Josh jerked Danny sideways and hissed at him to be quiet when he protested. Harry, Josh's nemesis and leader of the YHT, taller than the rest, lean and nasty, was heading their way.

Nipping in and out of the families clustered close to the parade route Josh and Danny finally made it into the relative safety of the middle of the crowd. Now that he had stopped running Josh felt his knees begin to shake. The events of the past hour crowded in on him and he steeled himself against the sudden nausea and shakes.

Danny was still trying to catch his breath as the girls of the school athletics team walked past, in their sleek outfits and short skirts. His eyes were squinting at all the bright colours and movement as if they hurt and everything was just too bright and garish. He looked hot and was sweating from the run through the town; far from looking inconspicuous he was bright red in the face. It was a dead giveaway.

Josh looked as if nothing was bothering him at all, but under his calm exterior he was struggling to get his stomach under control. The coppery smell of Ranj's blood seemed to be thick in his nostrils and catching at the back of his throat. As he thought about it he felt the gorge rising in his throat. He clenched his teeth and willed his thoughts away from the gory mess he had left behind, unconsciously wiping his hands against the legs of his jeans, again and again.

He stared at the parade, hardly able to make any sense of anything he saw until beyond the parade a familiar face stood out from the crowd at the far side. It was Skye. She saw him watching her and rolled her eyes at him. Josh had a moment of panic, thinking she knew what had just happened, before he realised he was being stupid. There was no way she could know.

He stared at her and again she scowled at the three girls leading the girls' athletic team. Skye thought they were lightweight and a real waste of space. And although Josh kind of agreed with her, he never admitted it, especially since Sandie, the star of the team, had been chatting him up recently. Josh had been pretty pleased with himself and knew it would do wonders for his street cred just being seen with her. In some ways that was what had started it all.

A couple of weeks before, Harry had been boasting all over the school about how Sandie fancied him, but he said she was too shy to show it. Josh thought she had never seemed very keen on Harry at all, although he knew better than to say anything. A few days later, right in front of most of their year, Sandie had told Harry to get real and leave her alone. Harry was blazing, and it hadn't helped that he'd seen Sandie chatting up Josh the very next day.

Harry was not the one to stand by and let Josh

move in on 'his' girl—even if she wasn't Harry's girl by any stretch of the imagination. Josh knew from that moment on Harry was going to make his life even more difficult than it was already, but he never really expected anything serious to happen.

The final marching band went by and as the crowds began to disperse Josh realised he wasn't feeling sick any more. A space cleared but when he turned to look for Danny a hand grabbed him by the shoulder and jerked him backwards.

He stared up into a pair of dark, brutal eyes. Harry was surrounded by three of his tribe, each dangerous in his own way but none as mean as Harry. The YHT were known for their viciousness, they were hard and uncompromising in their loyalty to their leader.

Josh felt his stomach clench. He and Danny were outnumbered again but he refused to let that intimidate him, and a glare in Danny's direction warned the other boy not to show his fear. Syd grabbed Danny's arm, twisting it up behind his back until Josh could see the pain in his friend's eyes.

Harry's hand pinched Josh's shoulder, hard. 'Where's your mate, Ranj?' Josh tried to shrug Harry's hand off but he just squeezed harder making Josh grunt. Syd sniggered but it was cut short when Harry glared at him.

Fighting to stay outwardly calm Josh swallowed

a surge of fear. He tried to concentrate on his anger, picturing what had happened to Ranj so that he could chase away the fear he always felt when Harry confronted him.

'My mate? Thought he was one of yours now, Harry?' Josh felt like he was betraying Ranj again as he said it, but in some ways it was true; they'd not been real mates for a while now.

'You ran off and left him.' Josh found himself short of breath and he wished his heart would stop thumping. He tried to stand taller as he faced up to Harry, hoping his knees wouldn't give way, but he held onto the anger deep inside and it seemed to give him courage. 'Thought you lot stuck together? He was one of yours—and you all just ran.'

Harry moved closer to Josh, his face inches away, his foul breath making Josh want to puke. 'So, where is he now?'

Josh swallowed, his muscles screaming in protest as he forced the upward edges of his mouth into more of a grimace than a grin. 'You know exactly where he is, Harry. Should've been you.' He was fighting to stay outwardly calm, swallowing a hot surge of rage and fear that mingled until he didn't know one from the other. 'He was one of your YHT. You think you're so hard, but you're all just yellow.'

Harry looked like he wanted to thump him but it was too public, something Josh had been counting on.

'We saw you do it.' Syd's eyes narrowed with the

threat, to make sure Josh understood the implication.

Harry glared at Syd.

Josh gave a sharp, high pitched laugh in Syd's direction and hoped that Danny didn't start to blubber. 'Who'd believe you, Syd? You wouldn't know your own mother if you saw her in the street.'

Syd's frustration showed on his face. He knew he couldn't do anything to get back at Josh; that was Harry's privilege and his alone, so he racked up the pressure on Danny's arm.

'Don't waste your time, Syd, Danny can take more than you can give out and you know it.'

Josh was thankful that his voice hadn't started to wobble but he knew there was only so much the YHT could do in such a public place. Already a few people had turned to watch them, and one man looked as if he might decide to interfere.

In the distance the sirens wailed. Was it the police or an ambulance? Even though they'd fallen out a long time back, Josh hoped it was for Ranj. He didn't like to think of him lying there, all alone.

Feeling the restlessness around them Harry nodded at the rest of the YHT and with a threatening, 'Gonna get you too, Josh. See if I don't!' they melted away into the crowd.

'Not if I see you first!' Josh called after them.

'Sod them,' Danny whined, massaging his sore shoulder.

But Josh wasn't listening. He was thinking about

Ranj. Harry's threats had almost become routine, but what had happened today had escalated it onto a different level. Josh could still hardly believe it had happened. Everyone around them was acting as if it was another normal day. He wanted to scream at them, that nothing was the same anymore. Ranj was gone.

He was DEAD!

Josh and Ranj had been mates, but that was before Ranj joined the YHT; before they had discovered knives and gangs; when they had been kids, buddies who shared secrets. He could picture the scene not far away, the lights, the police; the black bag zipped up with Ranj inside.

Josh felt the knife in his back pocket. He'd carried Gary's knife for a while now but he hadn't thought what he would feel like if he ever used it. It was what everyone did, carrying a knife, none of them really expected it to come to this. It was just for security, for protection, no more than a threat.

But why had it been Ranj? Why couldn't it have been someone like Harry? Josh didn't think he would mind if it had been Harry. He was almost sure he wouldn't have minded at all, or would he? But suddenly he remembered how it felt as the knife sliced into Ranj, all that blood. It wasn't what he expected at all and now he felt sick again just thinking about it.

People were starting to move around them and Danny was standing, waiting to be told what to do next. Josh suddenly felt tired. Why did he have to make all the decisions?

'C'mon, let's shift.'

Danny followed, still rubbing his shoulder. 'Where we goin', Josh?'

Josh shrugged and kept on walking. He needed to do something about the knife, to get rid of it somewhere no one would find it. Thinking about the knife made him think about Ranj, so he thought about Harry instead. He pictured Harry lying bleeding on the ground instead of Ranj. The more he thought about it the easier it was, and the more he believed it, the more his confidence was beginning to return. Yes, it would be cool. He would think of Harry zipped up in the black bag, dragged away stiff and lifeless. Maybe he could live with that, anything was better than thinking about Ranj.

I never knew there could be so much blood. It's everywhere, thick and so very red. Nothing I do seems to make it stop. My clothes are soaking it in now, becoming dark and wet.

'Josh, w-w-what d-d-do I d-d-d-do?' Danny only stutters when he's nervous. His voice squeaks, his eyes staring like two huge gobstoppers and I almost expect them to start spinning like a cartoon character's. I realise now that it's really too late for me, we're too far away to get help in time, I'll be gone soon. It's sort of inevitable, on a road with no turning back.

The blood just keeps on coming, making rivers in the dirt.

It's weird, I don't really care now it has actually happened, but Danny is still standing there looking terrified.

'Run, Danny, get away and don't tell anyone you were here. You know you can't be here. Your mum needs you at home.'

'B-b-but I can't j-just g-g-g-go. What ab-b-bout you?'

'Get out of here. There's nothing you can...aah... do. Just go!'

I try to move, to wave him away, but the movement shoots another dagger through my side. 'I'm a gonner, there's nothing you can do, so beat it!'

17

He stands there undecided, helpless, and looking more confused than usual. I take as much of a breath as I can and push all the anger I feel into it.

'I said, BEAT IT!'

I almost feel sorry for him as he steps back looking at me, before he turns and, as usual, does exactly what I've told him to do. 'You can tell them it was me, Danny, when they ask about Ranj. It makes no difference now.'

I'm alone now, all alone.

I can feel snowflakes falling on my face. It's a bit early for snow but it might even be a white Christmas, not that I'll see it.

TWO: Home

Sunday morning

When Josh got home he turned the key in the lock and pushed in through the door, looking forward to the chance to be alone. He needed time to think, to get his head straight. He knew his Mum would be at the Runaway Centre so he'd have plenty of time to get himself sorted.

As soon as he stepped into the hallway he realised he wasn't alone, his dad was back. He never knew when his dad would be home but he'd only been away a couple of days this time so Josh wasn't expecting him to be back so soon.

His dad came out of the kitchen. 'Where've you been?'

Josh swallowed. 'Out,' he snapped.

He knew his dad would give him a hard time for an answer like that but he didn't care. His dad stood staring at him and Josh stopped dead still when he realised he had been wiping his hands on his jeans again and again. Hardly able to breathe, he glanced down quickly to check, but the blood smears had dried to a dull brown, looking more like mud or dirt.

'It's the carnival in the park, Dad.' He tried to keep his voice casual as he ducked past his father and into the kitchen.

'Your mother's out at the Centre, then?'

Josh shrugged. 'S'pose so.'

'There's nothing in this house to eat,' his dad grumbled, opening and slamming the cupboard doors. 'I suppose she'll be there all day then? She's always there.'

His dad was right; mum was never at home, she was always at the Centre. Josh knew better than to say anything, it would just start another argument. Besides he agreed with his dad but somehow even that didn't seem to go down too well, either. He couldn't win. Helping himself to a can of coke from the fridge, Josh headed for his room.

'Where you off to now?' His dad was in a filthy mood but Josh knew he was only usually like that when he was tired and hungry. 'I work away all hours driving that truck and I come back here to an empty house. Don't know why I bother.'

'I'm going to get changed. I'm going out,' Josh said, heading for the stairs. 'Mum said she'd be back later, she said she wouldn't be late.'

In the safety of his room Josh slumped on the floor. He stared at his jeans where the blood had dried, Ranj's blood, leaving dark stains. He felt like his head was full of voices shouting, remembering, like a film running behind his eyes he could see Ranj and his look of surprise as the knife went in.

He never meant to use the knife, not really, he was just trying to protect himself, and if anyone it should have been Harry he cut, not Ranj. Why did Ranj end up in front of his knife? It was stupid...no, he couldn't think about that. He had to keep thinking about Harry, it was Harry's fault. He couldn't think about Ranj at all or he would lose it completely.

Josh shook his head as if to try and clear it. He had to get rid of the knife and fast, before anyone came looking and asking questions. He could imagine the police asking who Ranj's mates were. Ranj's mum would send them to Josh's house to see if he knew who had done it. She still thought they were as close as they used to be. She wouldn't know that things had changed between them. Ranj would never have told her.

He turned the knife over in his hands, inspecting it as if he'd never seen it before. It used to be a thing he was proud of. It had been Gary's knife, but now he could hardly bear to touch it. He used to love to polish the clean shining blade, the strong smooth silver handle, keeping it in good nick for Gary; when he came back. A stray, angry thought flitted past; that it had all been Gary's fault, if he hadn't left things might have been different; Josh and Ranj would still have been best mates and none of this would have happened. It seemed easier to blame Gary, to blame someone else. He threw the knife across the room and grabbed his head, pulling at his hair. He was losing it! He had to get himself together, get things sorted.

His hands smelt of blood, a metallic smell that

was almost a taste at the back of his throat. He had to get up and do something or he'd lose it altogether. He would wash his hands and his jeans; he had to get rid of the blood. What else did he have to do? He mustn't forget anything but his head was spinning and it was difficult to think straight.

How was he going to get rid of the knife? Where could he put it? Not in the house. Dig it into the garden? With his luck the neighbour's smelly dog would be there digging it up five minutes later. Josh could just imagine the scene: Mrs Banks fussing over her stupid dog and asking what he had found and then seeing there was blood on the knife, she would scream blue murder.

That wouldn't work. Could he throw it away? Maybe he could hide it in a skip, there was one down the road, it had been there for ages, or there was always the river, but what if it floated or just lay there. There had been a drought two years before and all sorts of things were found on the dry riverbed. Josh knew all about it because he had been one of those searching for anything they could find.

He could hide it in his dad's truck but that was too close to home and he didn't want his dad getting into trouble. That got him thinking. Could he toss it down from the overpass and try to get it into one of the trucks passing by? No, that was just plain stupid, he'd probably miss and someone would see him and the police would come to his house. The whole scenario played out in his head. He had to put it somewhere it wasn't going to be found easily or for a very long time. His mind wandered through the films he loved, where they buried bodies in cement, but he didn't know of anything being built...or did he?

That house with the skip outside, it was having all sorts of things done. If he could get in there tonight, maybe he could find a place behind a wall or something that would never be found, for years and years. By then no one would have any idea whose it was.

Josh wouldn't be sorry to lose it now. He used to like the knife because it was a kind of connection to Gary, but now he felt sick when he looked at it; at the dried blood on it, Ranj's blood. He'd done that. With a shake of his head he grabbed an old t-shirt, one he'd never liked anyway, picked up the knife and wrapped it up before heading to the bathroom.

Behind the locked door he ran the knife under hot water, steeling himself to stop the bile that rose in his throat at the sight and smell of the blood loosening from the blade. It had dried a dull reddish brown on the knife but was turning into a running red river as it washed away, following a sickly spiral down the drain. He rubbed at it until every speck of dried blood had gone and then he washed the handle too, scrubbing it with a nail-brush in the scalding water.

He had watched a lot of cop films and they seemed to be able to get all sorts of information from murder weapons...that thought stopped him.

Murder.

Was Ranj really dead? Could it really be true? He washed the knife again, rubbing it hard with his t-shirt until it was dry and the blade shone once more.

Satisfied that he had done as much as he could he wrapped it up again in the old t-shirt. Using a face cloth he tried to scrub the blood out of his jeans but it didn't work. The cloth took on the same muddied red colour and the more he rubbed his jeans the more blood came out. The wet cloth spattered pink spots onto the mirror and the sink. It was going everywhere. Suddenly he could see the spray of blood that had spattered the graffiti on the walls of the alley as he had jerked the knife back out of Ranj.

He slumped down onto the toilet seat as another wave of nausea rose up and he fought to keep it down. It was a few minutes before he could stand again and surveying the mess he realised he had to put his jeans in for a proper wash but he couldn't leave them for his mum to find. He took a few minutes to find the bathroom spray his mum used and carefully wiped away the spatters on the mirror and the sink before he hurried back to his room.

His dad had the TV on and he had probably

opened a couple of cans to drink while he watched the footie, so Josh knew he wouldn't come up and bother him.

Back in his room he found another pair of jeans that were almost clean, put them on and slipped the clean knife into his back pocket. He grabbed some other stuff to hide his jeans in and with an armful of washing he headed to the kitchen to set the machine going. It was just as well his mum was always giving him jobs to do in the house; at least she wouldn't wonder why he had put the washing on.

'I'm going out, Dad,' he shouted in the direction of the living room a few minutes later, only just loud enough to be heard over the TV. Grabbing his new leather jacket he dived out of the front door before his dad could object, or send him on some errand.

Outside Josh shrugged on his jacket and stuck his hand in the back pocket of his jeans, to make sure the knife was still there. Josh felt safe on the streets most of the time, except the part of town the YHT called their end; and although the knife had been part of his protection against the YHT, it now felt like a traitor in his pocket. It hadn't helped. It had been the cause of all his problems and now all he wanted was to get rid of it.

He had arranged to meet Danny back at the chipper and he'd made Danny swear not to say a single word to anyone, no matter what they said to him.

Danny was the weak link. He'd never rat on Josh, but at times he could be just plain careless and a cop with a single brain cell could run rings around him. Josh knew he was a bit rough on Danny, who had his own troubles.

Danny never said anything about it and Josh never asked, but he knew Danny had some kind of problems at home. He was always rushing back home as if he was terrified not to. Josh found it difficult to understand why Danny let it go on without doing something about it, if it was his dad or mum giving him grief.

Josh knew his own parents weren't the best in the world, as far as he was concerned, especially when there was anything going on that just might lead them to Gary; but Josh thought Danny's home life sucked even more than his did. At least Josh knew his parents would leave him to do pretty much what he wanted, they weren't really home often enough to demand that Josh came back early all the time.

'Hi Josh.' A quiet voice called to him from the doorway across the road and started him out of his thoughts.

'Skye!'

He really didn't want to speak to anyone, he had to get rid of the knife and get his story straight with Danny first.

Skye fancied him but although he liked her and they got on okay, he never thought about it being more that that. Josh could just imagine Harry making a lot of jokes about her and giving them both a real hard time if Josh had started going out with her. He made all sorts of excuses to himself, but underneath it part of Josh didn't want to admit that the real reason was because she wasn't exactly the kind of girl that gave him any street cred, not like Sandie. He buried that thought feeling slightly guilty. He and Skye got on really well when they met in cyberspace, chatting and playing on-line games. She was ace at Blitzer Dragonz, his favourite game of all time, and Josh struggled to beat her.

She wasn't really bad looking, just a bit nerdy; that weird thing she did, pulling at her sleeve to hide her arm all the time, didn't help. But right now he didn't want to stop and speak to her. He had other things on his mind.

'See ya later, Skye.'

Skye watched him walk away, then turned and went inside. She really liked Josh; he stood up to the bullies like Harry, who everyone knew was really pretty dangerous. Josh always seemed cool and unafraid. She thought he was kind of edgy and exciting—and a bit sad at times, too. Skye could relate to that.

He didn't speak to her all that much outside or at school but they chatted a lot online. She knew her Gran didn't like him very much, but underneath the cool exterior Skye could sense that he was kinder than most of the boys she knew; that was part of what attracted her to him.

• • •

Danny had gone straight home when he left Josh. He hurried to get there, he had no choice and knew he'd better get back before it got too late. His mum would be waiting.

He opened the door as quietly as he could and slipped his jacket off. He had just put the kettle on when he heard a noise and wandered through to the bedroom where he gently opened the blinds.

'Is that you, dear?' His mother's voice was a bit hoarse but cheery as usual although Danny knew she was constantly in pain.

'Yes, Mum. Sorry I'm a bit late.'

'Been out with your friends? That's what I like to hear. How is Josh?'

Danny made a face, thankful that his mother couldn't see it. He was hoping he could keep his voice happy or his mother would know something was up. She could usually tell when Danny had a secret or was trying too hard to hide one.

'He's fine, Mum. Anyway let's get you up. I'm making some food. Do you feel like sausages in gravy or just a little scrambled egg?'

'Just a little of whatever you are making will be fine, dear. You sound tired. I hope you've not fallen out with Josh? He seems such a nice boy.'

'No, Mum, Josh and I are fine, I'm just hungry, that's all. Here let me get your stick. Do you want to go through to the TV or come into the kitchen with me?'

'I'll go and sit by the TV, love.'

He helped his mum through, although she could manage without him if she had to, it took her ages to walk anywhere. He settled her onto the settee before he went to collect her pills and a glass of water. When she had taken them he put her knitting into her hands. Despite not being able to see very much at all, Danny knew his mum enjoyed listening to the TV and she loved knitting, so as long as Danny set out her wool in the right order to start with she managed to knit the most amazing scarves and jumpers just by the way the stitches felt.

Back in the kitchen Danny rushed about making some lunch for them both. He was quite a good cook, he had to be, his mum got really exhausted if she had to stand for more than a few minutes. She had been getting steadily worse over the last year so Danny had taken over more and more of the jobs that needed to be done around the house. He made sure that he managed to look after his mum but he was constantly worried that the social services would come and take her into one of those horrible nursing homes. He knew she would hate that, and then what would happen to him?

While he peeled onions and started chopping

them he wiped tears from his eyes with the back of his hand. He was glad the onions made his eyes water. He wanted to cry; he felt shaky when he remembered what had happened to Ranj.

He put the chopped onions into the pan but when he picked up the knife again it slipped and nicked his finger. The sight of blood on the knife turned his stomach and he dropped it with a clatter, running to the toilet to be sick. He retched until there was nothing left and slumped on the floor, his legs shaking so much they were unable to support him any longer.

He kept remembering Ranj on the ground and all that blood. It could have been him. He had seen the knife in Harry's hand. He could imagine how it would feel as it slipped into his own side, his imagination running away with itself until he could hardly breathe.

'Danny. Danny! Is everything all right in there? Where are you? I can smell something burning.'

Staggering to his feet he quickly splashed water on his face and rinsed out his mouth to wash away the acid taste of sick. Grabbing a breath to steady himself he shouted, 'It's okay, Mum.'

He ran back to the kitchen and turned the heat off under the frying pan, throwing the burnt onions into the bin, he got some more out to start again. His legs were still feeling wobbly but he managed to stumble through to the living room and put his head around the door.

His mother's face turned up towards him and once more Danny was grateful she couldn't see but he knew his mother realised something was wrong.

'You okay, love?' she asked gently.

Danny cleared his throat and forced a smile into his voice. 'I'm fine, mum, I was at the toilet and the onions got a bit burnt. But it's all fine now.'

Danny hated the fact that Josh carried a knife but he would never say anything. Josh was the one who made the decisions and being Josh's best mate was the best, most exciting thing that had happened to Danny since his mother had taken ill.

No one, not even Josh, knew that Danny did everything at home. He didn't want anyone to know. He was scared that if the social workers found out they would come in and take his mum away and they might even put Danny in a home, too, or with foster parents, because he was too young to live on his own and there was no one else to look after him. So he kept quiet and got on with things as well as he could.

He didn't mind looking after his mum but it meant that he never had much time for going out and he'd never had any real mates, until Josh came along. Danny never expected someone like Josh to want him around; he knew he wasn't quite as smart as Josh, or Ranj. Ranj had been Josh's best mate for years and Danny realised that he was just a kind of substitute, but he was so grateful to

Josh for letting him hang around with him that he didn't mind being second best.

By the time they find me will I be frozen into a statue, sitting in a pool of blood? The snow is heavier now and Christmas isn't far away.

I remember that last Christmas, how many years ago was it, when everything was great—all the family together—me, mum and dad, and Gary? It's like a warm cosy memory of someone else's. It's like one of those cheesy films they put on every year, the ones where all these perfect families have this amazing time and it snows and everyone cares about everyone else. Like on the TV where there are all these things that you can buy, except when there's not enough money of course, they never show that. It's all a bit sick really, no one believes it except the really little kids and they don't know any better. No one really lives like that. Christmas is just another excuse for being miserable in our house. I hate it.

That was the last one we had together. Ranj came round, too. He and his mum brought us cards and we all swapped presents. We'd made one of these silly childish pacts that we would always be mates. That didn't last either, nothing does. Ranj was as bad as the rest. He drifted away too. He didn't understand what it was really like in our house after Gary disappeared, no one did. How could they, unless it had happened to them?

After Gary was gone none of us really felt like

celebrating at all and we weren't like a family any more. Mum and Dad tried to make it right the next year but it was all such a sham, which was even worse. Everyone was pretending to be happy when it was patently obvious that we were all screwed up inside.

I like snow. It's cold and fragile, each flake different and it can just melt away when things get too warm for it. I feel like I am melting away. It hurts a bit, but not all that much. The puddle of blood beside me is getting bigger. At first the snowflakes were melting into it but now they are forming a covering on top. I can see through them and with the red of all my blood underneath the delicate patterns they look all Christmassy.

I should probably try to get up but when I move it hurts too much, and anyway what's the point, where would I go? It's too far to go home; I know I'd never make it. I can't feel my fingers anymore, I wonder if that's because of the cold or the loss of blood? I suppose I should try to move them but I'm not sure I can be bothered moving at all.

Perhaps someone will come and get me after all? Maybe Danny might have gone for help? I wish I wasn't here on my own. I wonder what it will be like to be dead. Will it just suddenly happen? I don't want to think about it now but I can't help it.

I don't want to die.

THREE: The Knife

Sunday afternoon

Danny was waiting by the fish and chip van, kicking stones across the pavement. Josh bought a bag of chips and they shared it, walking along the canal bank towards the old house. The canal was quiet with few people around at this time of year. In the summer the place was busy every weekend. Josh told Danny how he had decided to get rid of the knife and, predictably, Danny thought it was a great idea.

'All the workmen will be away over the weekend,' he told him as they headed towards the old house.

'But, what if the YHT turn up?' Danny looked around as if they would appear just because he said their name.

The YHT liked the canal, especially at this point where the buildings were more dilapidated and the weeds left to go wild. With less people around it was a good place to do business. Josh knew exactly what business they would be planning, and none of it boded well for him or Danny. They had to keep clear of them for a few days, to let the heat die down.

He bit his lip, thoughtfully. 'Heard anything about them finding Ranj?' he asked as casually as he could, to hide his concern. Taking some chips he crammed them into his mouth.

Danny shook his head, making his frizzy ginger fringe tumble into his face. 'Nothing yet. But I've not seen anyone really.'

'Me neither. There are less police around than I would have thought. Probably still trying to find their brains!'

Danny snorted and helped himself to a huge handful of chips.

'Thought you'd had your lunch? No wonder you can't run.'

Danny stopped dead. 'Sorry, Josh.'

He looked like a kicked spaniel. His big grey eyes and hangdog expression irritated Josh.

'Oh! You know I don't mean anything by it, Danny. I'm just hungry, that's all. It's been a day!'

Danny sniffed, but he handed back the last of the bag of chips. 'Yeah it has. Josh, d'you reckon Ranj's really bought it?'

Refusing to say anything Josh shrugged as if he didn't care at all. He didn't want to admit, even to himself, that Ranj was dead. 'Who knows? Who cares, anyway he got what he was asking for. I told him the YHT were a bad lot to get mixed up with.'

'But he was trying to help you.'

'Whose side are you on, Danny?' Josh yelled at him and raced off towards the metal fence that surrounded the work going on at the old house.

The fence was a series of tall wire rectangles about 15 feet high but only about 5 foot wide and in some places they were only joined together by a couple of pieces of tie-wire. Carefully choosing the weakest point, Josh crouched down and started to work on it until he could get two parts of the wire separated. It finally came apart, so he untied the broken ends and started on the next tie-wire above it.

Danny stood beside him, watching out for people coming past, but the lane was empty.

'Shouldn't we wait until later, when it gets dark?' Danny whined.

'Just shut up and keep watch.' Working out his anger on the wire it didn't take Josh long before he was pulling the fence apart to make enough space for them both to crawl through.

The site was covered in rubble, old bits of wood and other rubbish taken out of the house. They carefully picked their way to the far side of the building where there was a side door that was hidden from the public footpath and didn't look very secure. Josh slid his knife into the edge of the door and he and Danny pushed on it together to force the door open.

Inside they clambered over some old junk to get to the main part of the house.

'It's dark in here,' Danny muttered, 'I don't like it. I think this house is creepy.'

'Aw, Danny, button it, will you!'

'It's just that...'

'Just SHUT IT!' Josh couldn't take much more of his whining. 'Why don't you just go and wait outside? You can let me know if anyone comes along.'

'But if the YHT come I'd be on my own,' Danny moaned again.

Keeping his face turned away Josh clenched his teeth on a sharp reply. He couldn't afford to fall out with Danny, not now. There was too much to hide. He took a deep breath and tried to sound reasonable.

'Right. So for heaven's sake keep the flippin' noise down in case they do come. Just shut up and follow me. And don't touch anything, we don't want them thinking that there's been anyone in here, do we?'

Danny looked puzzled.

'Because they'll want to know what we were doing, Gonzo-head! And then they might find the knife.' Josh shook his head and pushed on through the house.

Inside, the wide hallway was clear of rubbish and to his left there was a short flight of stairs leading to a couple of rooms. A shaft of light caught the dust floating in the air but it only made the whole place look like something from a ghost story. Even Josh was beginning to get the jitters.

He could see that they had been working on the rooms upstairs because there were wooden planks running up the stairs to take the wheelbarrows up there. It looked promising.

Josh stopped. He turned quickly and put his hand over Danny's mouth before he could make a sound, indicating with his head towards the door they had used to get into the house. He held his breath until he could make out if the noise he had heard outside was people speaking.

It was the worst possible scenario. The YHT were outside the house, blocking their way out. He wasn't sure exactly where they were, but he thought they sounded quite close so they must have come through the opening in the fence. Josh knew he couldn't afford to get caught in such an isolated place, Harry's threats were not just hot air, he'd proved it that morning.

Josh signalled to Danny to start making his way quietly back towards the stairs, he needed to get to an upstairs window to see what was happening outside.

The sound of his heart thundering echoed in his ears as they stepped carefully across the floor and up the stairs. Every sound seemed like it was amplified, the creaking floors of the old house sounded like gunfire and at every step they were waiting for cries of discovery.

Up on the second floor Josh crouched down as he made his way towards the low windowsill. Down below he could hear the YHT and he reckoned they were probably sitting on the ground against the wall of the house. They would have decided it was a good place to have a smoke and a few cans, somewhere they wouldn't be disturbed and far enough from the main path, but Josh could feel his skin prickling as he realised they were directly below them.

From his vantage point he could hear everything that was being said, and that meant if he and Danny made any noise inside the house they might be able to hear them, too. Danny came and sat down below the sill next to Josh and they listened to Harry who was holding forth to the rest.

'How many are there?' mouthed Danny.

Josh held up all five fingers. Without Ranj that meant it was all of them.

'What about that Ranj, then?' Syd said, his voice softened and slurred by the drink.

'Yesh,' Joe's high pitched voice split the air like a siren. 'They thought he was a gonner when they found him, but I heard that they think he's going to make it. Shame you didn't just do it yourself, Harry.'

'Keep it down, will you, you stupid idiot,' Harry almost spat at him.

'I just meant that he wanted to save that little punk Josh, but he was supposed to be one of us. Got what he deserved, anyway. That's what I meant,' Joe put in quickly, trying to appease Harry.

'Yeah, right! As if,' Syd chimed in. 'What we gonna do about him, Harry?'

Josh curled his hand into a fist, wishing he was down there; he would show Syd. A wave of relief flooded through him. He realised that if Joe was right, it meant Ranj was still alive.

He wasn't a murderer.

He could think the word now without shying away from it, realising that it had been haunting him, unsaid, lurking at the edges of his mind. Things were working out better than he had thought possible. He would just have to dispose of the knife here and that would leave him in the clear.

Crawling away from the window Josh stood up as soon as he was sure he couldn't be seen from outside. Danny crept up beside him. Josh wanted to get out of the house but he still had to hide the knife. He stepped carefully over the rubbish on the floor and went to investigate one of the rooms on the other side of the house.

Here it was, just the place.

A wall was being built to cover some old stonework and although most of it was finished there was a single panel still to go on. Josh peered in behind it. There was just enough space to get the knife in behind the finished part of the wall and lots of insulation material to hide it in.

'This will do nicely,' he muttered, and threw the knife in as far as he could before collecting extra bits of insulation material to pack in the wall cavity so that it would hide the knife completely.

'Now, can you see it?'

Danny shook his head. 'I can't see nothin'.'

Josh almost felt like laughing out loud. He was rid of the knife and Ranj wasn't dead. Life wasn't so bad after all. 'Okay, let's get out of here.' It had all been so much easier than he had thought.

They couldn't go out of the door they had come in by and it looked like Harry and the rest would be at the back of the house for a while. Josh was impatient now to get away and leave it all behind him.

He led the way back to the ground floor and into one of the larger rooms at the front. Danny stumbled over a box in the darkness and let out an expletive.

Josh froze on the spot, waiting to see if they had been heard. They stood like moonlit marble statues waiting, waiting, hearts thumping and a look of horror frozen onto Danny's face. But there was no commotion, no outcry from outside.

'They're probably so spaced they couldn't hear if we yelled,' Josh whispered.

The old window had been replaced with a new one, which was a bit stiff but it finally opened with barely a squeak. Josh scrambled out and Danny tried to follow but Josh had to pull hard on his jacket to get him through the gap.

It was almost dark but with a full moon it was bright enough to let them see their way clearly to the road. At this side the house was directly on the road so there was no fence, which made it all much simpler. Josh breathed easier as they trotted away from the house and the YHT.

Danny started to gabble on about how close that

had been and how scared he had been but Josh tuned his voice out until it was just like a low buzz in his ear and easily ignored.

Josh was thinking. Trying to make sense of all that had happened since he had arrived at Jordan Alley that morning, when they had met up with Harry and the YHT poised for a fight.

'He did it on purpose!' Josh's outburst surprised even himself. 'Of course! It was a complete set up. Why didn't I see that before?'

He turned to Danny who was staring at him, stopped in mid sentence by Josh's comment. 'It's obvious, Danny. Harry set this whole thing up. He was conning Ranj into believing he was one of them, but all the time what Harry wanted was to use him to get at me!'

'What?' Danny was not following Josh's reasoning at all. 'What do you mean?'

They had just arrived at the kiddies play park and Josh sauntered over to the swings and sat down on one. Swinging his feet, he leaned back to feel the cool night air on his face as he pushed the swing up into the air, forcing it to go higher.

Danny slumped down on the other seat and started twisting himself round and round until the chains were tight all the way from the top bar to his head. He lifted his feet to let it spin until it was almost unwound, dragging his feet, and then started to do it again.

Josh forced himself higher and higher. Gary

used to take him to the swings when he was little, and pushed him until he yelled because it was too high. The thought of Gary made him feel depressed and he let the swing slow down again until he was just swaying back and forward, legs trawling the ground.

'Don't you see, Danny?' Josh said, continuing his earlier conversation. Danny thought Josh's voice was flat and icy, although someone who didn't know him might not have noticed. Danny hated when Josh was like this, stopping and starting, changing what he was talking about mid-sentence. It made him look stupid and he felt confused. He knew he wasn't as bright and clever as Josh, although most of the time Josh didn't seem to mind.

Josh didn't wait for Danny to answer. 'Harry's been looking for a way to get me for ages and he knows that Ranj and I knew each other since we were kids, so he decided to use that to get at both of us, the evil, conniving b—' Josh's expletives disappeared into the air as he pushed the swing higher again.

It was a few minutes before he was calm enough to speak rationally again.

'He set up that fight and used Ranj as the dummy. That's why they all left so quickly and didn't back Ranj up when he was hurt. They wanted him to get hurt! Well, either him or me. I don't suppose Harry gave a damn who it was.'

'Didn't he?' Danny was trying very hard not to

get left behind but he was struggling.

Josh jumped off his swing and turned to catch the chain supporting Danny's, so that he could look him in the eye.

'Because now that Ranj's been stabbed, it gives him every excuse to come after me, and anyone would back him up. To everyone else Ranj was one of the YHT, wasn't he?'

Danny watched as Josh's eyes narrowed into hard slivers. 'He didn't care if I killed Ranj, he's been planning this all along. He just wanted to get us both.' Josh started walking fast towards the road.

'Josh, wait for me,' Danny wailed, trying to untangle himself from the twisted chains of the swing. 'Where are we going, now?' he puffed as he finally caught up with him.

'Sorry, Danny, I have to do this alone.'

'Do what?'

'I have to go and see Ranj, and find out if he's okay. I've got to speak to him.'

'But they won't let you in to see him until tomorrow anyway...'

Josh shrugged, but he kept on walking.

Danny watched him walk away knowing that nothing he said would make any difference. He turned and headed home alone.

FOUR: Questions

Sunday afternoon

When Josh got home his mother was in the kitchen. He wondered if his dad had called her to say he was home. His mum was cooking and it was a familiar smell that normally felt home-like and comforting, but for some reason Josh found it cloying and sickly.

'Where've you been, Josh?'

He tensed, hearing the confrontation in her voice only mildly blanketed by her chatty conversational tone. His mum was about to start in on him and he didn't have the space in his head to deal with that.

'I was out with Danny.' *Deal with it*, Josh was thinking. He knew his mother would be irritated by his tone of voice but he didn't have the energy to do anything about it.

He watched her stirring the pot and pausing to add some spices to the curry she was making. Although it was usually his favourite and he'd not eaten much all day, the smell was turning his stomach. He headed for the door.

'Josh, wait a moment. Did you hear about Ranj? He's in hospital.'

It was like a game of chess. His mother's voice said she was trying not to get into an argument but that she was about to anyway. Josh was trying to decide how he should play it.

He wanted to go and see Ranj and it sounded like his mum had already been speaking to Ranj's parents. How much did they know? How much did his mother know?

Why was she trying so hard not to start an argument with Josh, all of a sudden? She'd hardly spent more than a few minutes speaking to him for ages. Josh couldn't remember how long for, other than the usual 'tidy your room' or 'what time of the night do you call this?' type of thing. His mum was always too busy and preoccupied with what was happening at the Centre to spend much time asking him what he was doing, not that he minded all that much, it made life easier. He could do pretty much what he wanted as long as he didn't stay out until the middle of the night.

'I heard about it.' Josh said, turning to go up stairs before his mum asked too many questions. 'Is he okay?'

'Someone stabbed him!' His mum stopped stirring and turned off the heat under the pot. Josh wanted to run upstairs but he was caught, stuck there wanting to know more but desperately trying to avoid the conversation that was coming.

The knife was gone. He had to remember that and he knew that none of the YHT would grass him up. At least that was what he would have thought normally, but Syd's words came back to him. They wouldn't grass on him would they?

They spoke to no one outside of their gang, did they? But the threat hung in the air like some dark shadow above his head.

'Is Ranj okay?' Josh asked again, trying to keep his voice as normal as he could. But what was normal?

Normal for a person who was concerned about a mate he had been on opposite sides from ever since...whenever, for a year at least?

Normal for someone who didn't want to tell his mother that he had just stabbed someone?

Normal for someone who knew the person he had stabbed had just been trying to help him after all?

Normal for someone who was so angry that he had been manipulated?

That was what made Josh's insides clench. His stomach felt like it was so empty his insides were sticking together like thin pieces of paper.

'He's not 'OKAY'!' Now his mother was getting angry. Josh realised she suspected he knew something he wasn't telling her. Surely Ranj wouldn't have pointed the finger at him, would he?

'He could have died!' Her voice was high and shrill.

'I know that, Mum. I just meant...'

'You know something about it, don't you!'

It wasn't really a question and Josh's mind was racing trying to find a way out of it. A hundred questions with no answers were crowding out his head.

'The police were here, asking questions. They wanted to know where you were, and of course your dad had no idea. He said you'd come in and gone out again this morning.'

'The police?' Josh felt as though he had been thumped in the chest and all the breath had been forced out of his lungs.

'What happened to your jeans that you put them in the wash? I only put them up in your room yesterday. They were clean then but when I took them out of the wash they had some dark marks on them.'

'I've got to go.' Josh started to make for the front door but his mother caught his arm before he reached it.

'No, you're not going anywhere until you tell me what happened today, and where you were.'

Allowing himself to be led back into the kitchen, Josh felt limp and exhausted. His mother knew something, but what exactly did she know? Her next words were more confusing than ever.

'Ranj asked to see you, and the police want to speak to you, too, because you're his best friend. We've to go to the police station after we've been in to see Ranj. I told his mother that I would bring you into the hospital after tea. He kept saying he wanted to see you.'

'Do I have to?' Josh couldn't face seeing Ranj, even though less than half an hour before he had thought that was exactly what he did want to do. He was suddenly reluctant to face him.

His mother looked as if she was having trouble controlling herself.

'Do you *have* to? I know you've not been as close to Ranj these last few months but the poor boy almost died today. I thought you'd be keen to go and see him.'

'Whatever!' Suddenly all the bitterness and resentment Josh had kept to himself for far too long started to spew out over his lips like a revolting floodtide of rotten feelings. 'How would you know anything about what I want, anyway?'

The words were out before Josh could stop them. 'You've not paid any attention to anything I've said or done for ages, except when it involved Gary. Ever since he disappeared it's been Gary this, and Gary that. You spend all your time and loads of money trying to find him and looking for anyone who has seen him.' Josh picked up an orange from the bowl and squashed it between his hands as he spoke; digging his nails into the rind and feeling it slide under them in little orange flakes.

'If I wanted to go somewhere or do anything there was never time or money, but if pretty much anyone came along and said they might have seen Gary, that was different. There was always time and money to go and check it out, even if they were absolute loonies.' Josh plunged his thumbnail deep into the orange until he felt the juices squirt out and run over his fingers. The sharp citrus smell rose into the air between them.

'Didn't it ever occur to you to think about why he left? He never wanted to go to university or anything like that. All he ever wanted was to be in a band and you never listened. Perhaps he doesn't want to come back. Maybe he's happier wherever he is, away from you and this house. I know I would be!'

He ran out of things to say very suddenly and the silence that remained was like a huge space between him and his mother, opening out a yawning chasm that was growing deeper by the moment. He waited for her to retaliate, this silence was not like her at all. His dad was the one who usually used silence as a way of making you think about what you said, but his mother was the 'stand up and argue' type of person. Why was she so quiet now?

'I think you've said quite enough, young man.' His father's voice flowed into the room like a dark blanket of calm after a wild storm. 'Go up to your room and stay there. I don't want to see you down here until your tea is out and you'd better be ready to go straight to the hospital afterwards.'

Josh left the room without looking at either of them. He just managed to resist slamming the door behind him.

Up in his bedroom he turned on his computer.

There was an email from Skye. She was always at her computer and they spoke more online than they did face to face, which suited Josh fine. She was such a nerd; everyone knew she was brilliant and brainy but just a bit weird. What was bizarre was her screen name was WILDCAT—not the kind of name he'd have thought she would choose.

Online they really got on well. He struggled to beat her at Blitzer Dragonz, but he also found he could say things to her that he never told anyone else, like what he'd just said to his mum about Gary.

SPIKE *writes*
she knows its the truth

WILDCAT *writes*
doesn't mean yr mum wants to hear u say it

SPIKE *writes*
suppose. i felt better 4 saying it. been wanting 2 say it 4 ages.

WILDCAT *writes*
u all going 2 the hospital?

SPIKE *writes*
they want me 2. don't know what to do. i'm scared.

WILDCAT *writes*
what? u...never! anyway nothing bad's going 2 happen

SPIKE *writes*
he's been asking for me no one else, just me.

WILDCAT *writes*
Ranj wants to see u coz u r his oldest mate.

WILDCAT *writes*
u still there?

WILDCAT *writes*
HELLO??

SPIKE *writes*
yup. i'm here.

SPIKE *writes*
i still don't want 2 go.

WILDCAT *writes*
think what u would want if u were lying there in the hospital.

SPIKE *writes*
suppose...

WILDCAT *writes*
wouldn't have asked if he didn't want to see u. people who are ill rarely have energy to be bothered with people they don't like!

SPIKE *writes*
maybe

WILDCAT *writes*
definitely!

SPIKE *writes*
so—u playing Blitzer or just wittering on about other stuff all night? scared I'll beat u?

WILDCAT *writes*
dream on. I can wipe the floor with u anytime.

SPIKE *writes*
u'r on!

Josh always felt better after talking to Skye. She seemed to know what he needed to hear and then didn't go on too long about it.

It's cold and lonely, all on my own here, and it's getting dark now. I wish I'd not told Danny to go away. I know that it's better for him but the pain in my side is worse. It really hurts now and I hate being here all on my own.

I could have called my dad, like I used to when I was a kid. Whenever I was upset or hurt he'd be there in a minute, fussing and picking me up in his arms like I was a feather and weighed nothing at all.

But I don't want him to see me like this, he wouldn't understand. He rarely speaks to me, or mum, these days except to get angry, but then he's away off driving his truck most of the time, anyway. I think he hates to come home now. It's like he's running away. I'd like to run away, except I have nowhere else to go.

I tried to run away once, when Gary first disappeared. That was the first time I met Skye. I ran across the road and down the lane, running at full tilt, practically blind because I was trying not to cry but I couldn't help it. I remember feeling that if I ran far and fast enough I would leave it all behind and things would be like they used to be.

Mum and Dad had turned into these strange people who spent all their time on the phone or speaking to people about Gary. The police had been to the house and all sorts of people had turned up at the door asking about him.

I think Gary had been planning it for a while, saving up his money and then he just decided he'd had enough. Mum and dad would never let him do what he wanted with his life, so he left. But no one really cared what I thought. They asked me, then ignored what I told them.

I think I hated Gary for a while—for not telling me or asking me to go with him; for not coming home again or even leaving a note; for making my life less important because all that mattered to everyone was where Gary was.

I never believed that he was dead, not then and not now, either.

So I ran away. I ran as fast as I could, with no idea where I was going, no plan, I just wanted to leave these feelings behind. Suddenly I ran into a wall. It wasn't really a wall; it was a person, Skye.

She grabbed me to stop me knocking her over and we both almost fell. There was a bit of scrambling around until we found some kind of balance again and then for some reason we both started laughing.

'Hey, watch where you're going!' she said, with that quirky smile she has. 'You okay?'

I nodded, turning away and wiping my eyes on my sleeve so she wouldn't see I'd been crying, but she wasn't fooled. I was grateful that she ignored it, and somehow we just started walking and talking. In the end I went back home again. I realised there was no *point running away; I had nowhere else to go.*

Mum was frantic and started going on at me about how thoughtless I had been running off, didn't she have enough to worry about with Gary's disappearance? She never once asked how I was feeling. He's my brother and I was worried about him too, but that didn't seem to matter. No one cared what I was feeling as long as I just stayed at home and didn't cause any problems.

Skye had just moved in across the road and for a while she and I used to bump into each other outside in the street. She always started talking first, telling me about this weird programme on her computer or the latest game she was playing on it. She is pretty amazing, for a girl, and had created all these really weird creatures. She's a bit nerdy, going to the chess club and things like that, but get her talking about gaming and she is pretty switched on.

She has this crushed hand that she keeps trying to hide. I told her just to let it show; that no one would bother. She looks much more obvious trying to hide it all the time. It almost looks like she has a twitch!

When it became known that Gary had disappeared, people who knew us used to stop me in the street and ask if there was any news, but there never was. Skye said I shouldn't bother about it but I've always hated it. It's like I don't exist, they just want to know about Gary. I sometimes feel like saying 'No, we don't know where Gary is but, hello! I'm here!'

Probably no one will care that I'm dead, but at least they will know where I am and they can all still keep looking for Gary.

FIVE: Gary

3 years previously

It was a day like any other, the day Josh's life changed forever. There wasn't anything he did or could have done to change it. It just happened and things were never the same afterwards.

It was summer, the start of the holidays, and he had been keen to sleep late because he knew he didn't have to get up for school. The front door had a particular creaking sound when it opened and Josh later decided that was what had woken him up so early. His alarm clock showed 6.15am—the middle of the night as far as Josh was concerned. He turned over and disappeared into a deep, thick dreamless slumber.

The only time there was a noise that early in the morning was when his dad left early to go on some long trip, but he'd left the day before to take his lorry to Germany, so he wouldn't be back for a while. None of that registered until much later when Josh was trying to remember exactly what had happened.

It seemed like just a moment later when his mother pulled the curtains wide, letting painfully bright sunlight into the room.

'Mum!' he complained, in a voice thick with sleep.

'Josh, do you know where Gary is?'

He thought afterwards that something in the cosmic mists should have warned him that this was a question that would be asked of him repeatedly for the next few years, but such things don't happen. Josh mumbled a negative and pulled his covers over his head.

'Josh!' His mother's voice was unusually strident. 'Gary's not in his room. Did he say where he was going today?'

'No, Mum. He never tells me anything.' Josh mumbled from under the comfort of the bedclothes. 'He's probably gone to meet up with Kyle and Jack, or something. I want to sleep, Mum. It's the holidays.'

His mother went downstairs and Josh slipped back to sleep.

It was nearly lunchtime when he eventually surfaced and bleary-eyed he moped downstairs for some breakfast. His mother was usually at work by this time so he was surprised to see her still there, speaking urgently on the phone.

When she put the phone down she started asking him again if he knew where Gary might be.

'Why? What's he done?'

'He's gone. He left this morning or maybe last night, and he seems to have taken a lot of his things with him, his guitar and some of his clothes.'

'He's probably gone to Jack's to have a jam session or something.' Josh couldn't see what all the fuss was about. Gary had just finished his exams a couple of weeks before and had been hanging around the house ever since, when he wasn't out with his mates. They'd got together to form a band and all Gary wanted to do was to spend all his time playing guitar, writing songs and singing with them.

'Did he say anything to you after his argument with your dad the other day?'

'Mum, Gary never tells me anything. What are you so worried about? He'll be back later.' Josh helped himself to some cereal and sat down beside the TV to eat it.

His mum came and sat down opposite him, turning the TV off.

'Aw, mum, I was watching that.'

'Josh, I think Gary has left home. I think he's run away.' She stood up and paced across the room in front of him, she seemed unable to sit or stand still for more than a moment. 'I need to know if he said anything to you, anything at all. Jack and Kyle have no idea where he is but I know he was very upset the other day.'

'No, Mum. I told you, he never tells me anything.'

Josh could see how worried his mother was but he really didn't believe that Gary had gone, not really gone. He remembered the fight between Gary and his dad just before his father left for Germany. It had been a stinker of an argument, but that wasn't unusual, they were always arguing.

Later, when his mother had gone out, Josh went

out to meet up with Ranj.

'Where do you think he's gone?' Ranj asked, when Josh told him about Gary.

Josh shrugged. 'No idea. I just think Mum's having a fit over nothing. It'll all blow over by tonight. Gary was seriously peed off with dad and mum going on about him not studying enough and 'wasting his potential'. That's dad's favourite one, I think they imagine he's going to be a nuclear scientist and win the Nobel Prize or something. They're always giving him a hard time when he says he doesn't want to do what they want. They say he's wasting his time playing music with the band because it will never amount to anything.'

'Their band is pretty good, isn't it? They went down really well at the school charity thing. It'd be really cool if they cut a disc and became famous on a talent show on TV or something. Then your mum and dad would stop giving him such a hard time.'

'Yeah,' Josh plucked at an imaginary guitar and made accompanying noises. 'Like that's ever likely to happen!'

That night when Gary still hadn't come home his mum called his dad and told him that Gary had gone. She had spoken to all his friends but no one had seen him since the day before. His mum called the police and Josh heard her getting really ratty with them on the phone, but they said he was probably just away with his mates and to call back if he still wasn't home in the morning.

Josh went upstairs and pushed open Gary's door, almost expecting Gary to shout at him to go away. There was a bleak emptiness about the room. Gary's things were still scattered about but the most telling thing was that his guitar had gone. Josh knew that Gary would never leave it behind if he was going anywhere for long. It was almost permanently attached to him. His favourite long coat was gone, too. Josh went to have a look at Gary's desk, he still felt it was wrong to be here looking in the cupboards and drawers, and he knew Gary would give him a hard time if he found Josh messing about with his things.

Out of the corner of his eye Josh noticed something on the bed half covered by the bedclothes. Josh recognised the bright colours of Gary's secret stash box, where he kept his money and things he wanted hidden from their parents, and from Josh, of course. Gary thought no one knew about it but Josh had seen him opening it a couple of weeks before, when his bedroom door hadn't been completely closed. The box had been full of money, notes mostly so it must have been quite a lot.

Josh picked up the box, it felt too light and when he shook it nothing rattled inside. He was sure that was a bad sign. The money Gary was saving had probably come from birthday presents and his part-time job at the local supermarket and Josh assumed that he was saving it up to buy something special, another guitar or something like that.

Josh prised the lid open and the empty box shone back at him. A heavy feeling was growing in the pit of his stomach. Perhaps his mum was right. Maybe Gary *had* run away.

They fought a lot but no more than other brothers and Josh always knew that if he really needed something Gary would be there. But what if he didn't come back? Josh picked up the lid and closed the box again, pressing down hard as if that would somehow magic the contents into appearing again.

He felt empty. What if Gary didn't come back? Why hadn't he told Josh anything about what he was planning to do.

'What's that?' His mum came in and sat down on the bed beside him.

'It's Gary's money box. He usually keeps it hidden away, but it's empty. Mum, do you really think Gary's gone? Where would he go?'

She turned away and took out a tissue to blow her nose. 'I don't know, Josh. Perhaps he's just gone to buy something and he'll be back tonight.'

But Josh knew she didn't believe it any more than he did. The room had an abandoned feel, difficult to say why, but Josh felt as if it no longer belonged to Gary at all.

The next few weeks were the strangest in Josh's life. His dad came home and stayed there the whole time, it seemed like his mum was constantly crying.

Everything revolved around Gary's disappearance, every minute of the day. The police eventually agreed that he was missing and started interviewing his friends and Josh, but no one seemed to know anything. Josh got out of the house as much as he could, spending time at Ranj's house or out, anywhere but home.

If Ranj was here...

If he was here he'd be saying stupid things and making me laugh. We used to laugh a lot together, but after Gary left Ranj seemed to think I could just forget all about him really quickly and that things should just be back to normal.

He just didn't understand what it was like for me. It was a complete nightmare and it just went on and on. It was okay for Ranj, his life was the same, his parents were still the same and his little brother and sister. At his home things were like they had always been, but my life had changed completely. No one in my house was acting normally and more than anything I just wanted it all to go back to the way it was. I'm not even sure that I really wanted Gary to come home after that, because things never go back to being exactly how they were before; do they?

By the time Gary had been away for a year Mum had left her job at the supermarket and was spending all her time at the Runaway Centre. She was so completely engrossed with things there that she barely had time to do anything at home. She was always rushing back to the Centre to deal with some emergency or other and leaving me messages about getting my own tea or doing my homework. Dad started taking on longer trips away, so he was only home now and then. I didn't see any reason to spend time at home either; there was no one there most of the time.

But Ranj never understood what it was like or how much my life had changed and he expected me just to forget about it all. That made me angry with him. He should have known how bad it was for me; he should have understood. So I started hanging about with Danny and I know Ranj wasn't happy but I didn't care all that much. In fact I didn't care about anyone really. Why should I, no one seemed to care what was happening to me?

Poor Danny. I sometimes feel quite bad that I always give him such a hard time, always bossing him around. It just takes him so long to catch on to things, but I suppose he can't help it and he always agrees without question when I say something. At times that drives me crazy, too. Ranj would at least argue with me when he didn't want do something.

I feel sick. If I just shut my eyes for a bit it might help but I'm scared of falling asleep. Don't they say that when you go to sleep you just fade away and die?

I don't want to die but I'm really tired, maybe if I just shut them for a moment...

NO! I can't...I can't breathe, I can't seem to get enough air. Is this it? Am I dying right now? Ohmigod, ohmigod! No! NO!

No, I mustn't panic. I need to calm down, someone will come, they will—won't they?

If I count each breath, that might help.
One-two-three-four-five...
S l o w e r!
Six.
Breathe in. And breathe out.
Seven...

SIX: Ranj and the YHT

Ranj didn't like hospitals. He'd hated them ever since he'd been a child. He found them scary. He was in a ward with lots of old men and one of them was constantly shouting out at the top of his voice, jerking him awake whenever he fell asleep. It had scared him half to death the first time. It was as if the old man waited until the ward was completely quiet, and then screamed at the top of his voice. Not a scream really, just words, nothing that made any sense at all. He did it two or three times and then the nurse came along and he was quiet for a bit until Ranj had just fallen asleep, again, then it started again and woke him up. Weird old bloke!

Ranj was lying there thinking about Josh.

It had been a long time since they'd fallen out, but Ranj still thought of Josh as his best mate, no matter what had passed between them. He was feeling really groggy and had hardly even been awake when his mum came to visit but he remembered that he had told her he wanted to speak to Josh.

Ranj wished he'd never joined the YHT. It was partly Josh's fault. Josh had stopped speaking to him and started hanging around with Danny instead.

He'd been sitting on his own in the school cafeteria that day when Harry came up to his table.

'Not got your minder with you, then?' he sneered.

Ranj ignored him at first, but Harry didn't move, he just stood there. 'So where's Josh then, Ranj?' he asked.

Ranj shrugged, feeling more miserable than ever. He was jealous of Danny having taken his place as Josh's mate and part of him hated Josh for leaving him out of everything.

'How should I know?'

'Had a falling out, have we?'

Syd and the rest of the YHT slouched over with their trays to the next table and started making silly remarks, laughing at him.

Harry turned and glared at them. 'Shut it, you lot.'

He clipped a chair out from under the table with his foot, put his tray on the table and sat down across from Ranj. Expecting another mouthful of abuse or sarcasm Ranj continued with his lunch, trying to pretend Harry wasn't there.

'So you really want to sit here on your own?' Harry was shovelling baked beans into his mouth as he spoke.

Ranj thought it was just the start of another round of taunting. He knew how it went. Harry would ask him over to their table then trip him up or spill his lunch over him to make Ranj look stupid and get a laugh from his mates at Ranj's expense.

Not willing to play his part in Harry's cruel game Ranj just shrugged again.

'Sit with us. We're lookin' for someone like you to join the YHT. We need new blood and we're not interested in any of that lot over there.'

Ranj glanced back to see who was sitting behind them, wondering if Harry was just making a fool of him, but he looked as if he was being genuine, not what he'd expected to see on Harry's face.

'Why me?' Ranj couldn't resist asking the question but he wasn't sure he wanted to hear the answer.

'We're one short now that Jack's gone,' Harry said, looking Ranj straight in the eye. Jack had been excluded and finally chucked out for good, it had been the talk of the school before the summer holidays. 'You'd have to pass the initiation ceremony if you want to be one of us.'

'What's that?'

'You'll find out. Shouldn't be anything you can't handle, if you've got the bottle? You coming?' he asked again, indicating the other table where the YHT were.

'Why not!' All Ranj could think about, as he stood up with his tray, was what Josh would say if he'd seen him just talking to Harry, far less sitting with him and the rest of the YHT. All at once Ranj realised that Josh didn't care about where he was or what he was doing, so why shouldn't he join them?

'Ranj here is going to join the YHT,' Harry announced. He made a sharp negative with his head when Syd looked as if he was going to complain and the rest of them looked confused, but Harry was not someone they were prepared to disagree with.

One moment Ranj was scared of Harry and the YHT and the next he was going to be one of them. It had made him feel great to be in one of the most feared gangs in the school. Great, even if somewhere inside he wondered if it was a good idea. The initiation ceremony was bound to be something scary but he had clamped down fiercely on the voice inside telling him that this was not a good idea.

It felt good. It felt right. Why shouldn't he be part of a gang, and have some fun? They wanted him. It would show Josh.

SEVEN: The Fight

Ranj realised later that he should have known there was something serious going down on Sunday morning when Harry had been so very keen that he stayed close to him. Harry wouldn't tell him what they were going to do. He had sent some of the others away without saying where they were going, but Ranj noticed Harry and Syd sharing some secret glances that he wasn't meant to see, and that began to make him feel uneasy.

As it got later it was obvious they were waiting and looking for something, or someone? No one would answer any of his questions and Ranj was about to say he was going home; he felt really tense and Harry was looking far too smug.

When Josh and Danny came down the lane towards them he knew it was not going to be good. Ranj wished he had stayed at home that morning. Something bad was going down and he was trapped in the middle of it all.

Josh was chatting away and showing Danny something he had in his hand, completely oblivious to the fact that the YHT were there waiting for them, until it was too late. He saw Josh look behind him and that was when Ranj realised where the other two YHT, the ones who had been sent off earlier, had gone.

It was a trap.

Ranj had begun to hate Josh for the way he snubbed him all the time, even more so since he'd joined the YHT, and he was pretty sure the feeling was mutual. But despite being angry with Josh, Ranj didn't want anything to happen to him. Not anything serious, that is. He had a very bad feeling about what was happening. It had obviously been carefully planned but no one had told him anything about it.

There had been a kind of buzz with the rest of the YHT all morning. Harry wanted to get back at Josh, it was all he ever talked about, and now he had him trapped. Ranj knew Josh would try to talk his way out of it; it was the kind of thing Josh would do, but his gut feeling was that this would turn into something much more serious and Harry wouldn't be interested in talking.

Harry planted himself in front of Danny and Josh and drew out a long blade. 'What do we have here? A couple of little worms just ready for slicing up.'

When Josh looked up Ranj saw a flicker of fear cross his eyes but then it was gone and he wondered if he'd imagined it.

Josh lifted one eyebrow. 'You crawled out from under that stone early this morning, Harry!'

Ranj felt his stomach churning; this was not going to go well, he could sense the tension in the air, crackling between them. Josh was trying to bluff his way out of it but Ranj felt as if time had slowed.

He had a buzzing in his head that almost blotted out what they were saying, like one of those films when the sound slows down so that the voices sound deep and thick.

In Josh's hand a smaller knife appeared, almost by magic. But Ranj knew Josh, he was sure he would do anything rather than use it. It was just for show. Harry had his intentions clearly stated in the way he was standing and the threat in his voice. He wanted to do this; he had planned it and was not having a second thought. Josh was here and Harry meant him serious harm; that was plainly obvious to all of them.

Ranj wanted to shout at Josh, 'It's no use. He's not listening to you. He wants this to happen! RUN, Josh!'

But the words refused to come.

He thought it was strange to be watching and doing nothing, but it was as if part of him could already see what was going to happen long before it actually did. A kind of premonition.

Ranj saw the boys behind Josh and Danny moving in closer. Just as Harry was about to lunge at Josh, he turned and looked straight at Ranj, as if to boast that he was going to knife Josh right there and then, in front of him. Taunting him with his cowardice, to watch or do something about it. Harry was so sure he knew Ranj well enough that he was certain he wouldn't do anything to stop it.

Ranj knew he couldn't let it happen. Even afterwards, he had no idea why he'd done it, or what he thought he could do to stop it happening but as Harry waited a moment before moving in with the knife—Ranj rushed forward.

He'd been turning it over and over in his head as he lay in the hospital and it still just replayed again and again. Harry waited until Ranj got in front of him and then he pushed him hard forwards, towards Josh, onto Josh's knife. Josh looked stunned as he watched the knife in his hand slice into Ranj.

Even with his eyes shut Ranj could still see Josh; eyes staring, wide open, the handle of his knife still in his hand and the blade buried deep inside Ranj.

Ranj remembered how it felt as he slumped forwards into Josh's arms, the pain, dull at first then spiking sharp. He remembered falling because his legs couldn't hold him, and he hit the ground hard, like a bag of bones. That hurt, almost more than anything else.

When he closed his eyes Ranj could still hear Danny yelling.

It's freezing and it's getting pretty dark now. I don't really like the dark, I never have. When I was little and had nightmares Gary used to come into my room and leave his robot beside the bed. It was a weird looking thing but it had a red light that glowed out of the top of its feet, and that was just enough light to make me feel safe.

I wonder what happened to that robot. I'd forgotten about it until now.

It's just plain silly, lying here like this. I have things I wanted to do with my life. I thought I'd have lots of time to think about it, never thought it would come to this.

When I was little I used to want to be an explorer, until I discovered that you had to do things like climb mountains or go to the North Pole where it is really cold, or go through jungles where there were all these nasty biting insects that could kill you with one bite, or huge scary animals. What a wimp! I suppose I wasn't really cut out to be an explorer after all.

Ouch! I mustn't laugh it hurts too much.

Skye says she wants to work for NASA. She wants to go off to the moon or the other planets; sees herself as some kind of astronaut I suppose. She's probably brainy enough to do something like that. I can imagine her inventing a spacesuit that keeps you young so that you can travel for light years and not get any older, or some kind of space machine that translates alien languages.

I really don't know what I want to do but it doesn't really matter now because it's not going to happen, is it? I never thought this could happen to me, I suppose you never think it will be you, well, at least I never did.

Even when Gary couldn't be found and Mum thought he might be dead (not that she ever said it out loud, but I knew that was what she was thinking—but not thinking—if you know what I mean). Even then I never thought about what it would be like to die. I mean to really die—and not be here any more.

If I heard that someone had died I used to think, 'So what?', as if it didn't matter. But it matters. It really does matter.

I know I'm dying and I've only got—what is it now, I can just see my watch—probably less than 17 minutes? I know that because I watched this film on one of the information channels about how long it takes you to bleed to death. I think it might be different depending on where you are bleeding from, but I'm pretty sure it's only around 25 minutes max, so it could be even less.

I thought I would have plenty of time to get myself straightened out when I was older. I was going to go to Art College or maybe travel for a bit; go on a long trek and work my way around the world.

You hear about all these amazing places where you have a great time and maybe ride on a camel or an elephant or go to visit a pharaoh's tomb in Egypt. It would be ace. I was going to do all that—wasn't I?

I used to think I wanted to be a pilot and fly a jet, maybe join the air force. I could be a top fighter pilot. I know I could do that; it would be great.

Who am I kidding? It really doesn't matter now, does it?

Mum was really furious when she heard I had been there when Ranj was stabbed. I wasn't expecting her to be at home that day at all and that threw me. I wasn't ready to answer her questions. You never know what to expect with mum.

It was like that time I came home from school and found her just sitting there—crying.

EIGHT: The Body

It had been three months earlier, just another ordinary day no better than the one before it, probably worse if he admitted it. Josh had opened the front door and slung his bag down as usual, kicking off his shoes. The house was quiet; usually his mum had the radio on, or the TV if she was in. He called out but there was no answer so he assumed she was out, probably still at the Centre.

The kitchen was empty but when he pushed open the living room door, hoping to find his mobile on the coffee table where he'd left it that morning, he got a shock. There was his mother sitting on the sofa, not making a sound, not moving, just staring at nothing. She didn't even look round when he came into the room.

'Mum?'

She just sat there clutching a damp, scrunched up tissue, her eyes swollen blurs of red dampness. She didn't seem to notice that he was there. He tried to ask her a few times but she just ignored him with the occasional tear rolling down her cheeks and dropping unnoticed onto her hand.

Josh felt totally helpless, and angry. He'd had a rotten day at school and here was his mother sitting there, not even trying to tell him what was wrong.

He slammed the door of the living room and

stamped his way upstairs. His bedroom door got the same treatment and in a moment the house rocked with the full on blast of his music system. He knew that would irritate his mother and he expected some kind of immediate response but a full five minutes went by and Josh realised his mother had not even made the effort to shout up at him to turn it down.

What a useless mother she was, never there when she was needed and she didn't care what happened to Josh or what kind of bad day he'd had.

His mother usually wasn't even at home when he got there and now she was ignoring him, not even taking any notice whether he was there at all. She didn't care.

Underneath the anger Josh realised that it was probably something to do with Gary. It was always about Gary, it was all his mum cared about these days. Josh was used to the misery in his mother's voice when some initiative or other had failed to turn up any new information about him. He was sick to death of hearing about Gary.

Gary had gone. He didn't want to be part of the family any more. He had decided to leave without telling them anything—so stuff Gary!

It was almost two hours later when Josh finally emerged from his room. He was hungry and wondered if his mother had gone out of the house and not bothered to tell him. There were none of the usual sounds from the kitchen, no bashing of pots or crockery. In fact now that the pounding beat of his music had been turned off the house seem still, unnaturally so. Josh came down the stairs feeling like someone from a bad horror movie, half expecting the house to have been invaded by zombies.

His mother was still sitting where she had been when Josh left her. Still sobbing silently. He noticed that she was clutching something else in her hand beside the tissue. Josh was beginning to get scared now. What on earth could have made her react like this? Even for her this was something new. His first thought was what perhaps something had happened to his father. He knew his parents didn't get on like some picture book family but they always seemed okay. Had he had a crash with his truck, or something?

It couldn't be Gary. She was always obsessing about Gary but not like this, not since the first few months, when she was crying all the time. This was different.

The room was dark. The curtains hadn't been drawn and she had made no attempt to put on the light; it was as if she hadn't even noticed. Josh shivered. The house was cold so he turned up the thermostat and switched on the lamp on the table beside his mother.

Her hand was holding what looked like a crushed photo. Josh sat down beside her, he didn't know what else to do.

'What's wrong mum?' He said it quietly, it would

have seemed wrong to speak too loudly.

His mother sobbed but it was a painful dry sound that seemed to be rasping through her throat. She still didn't say anything, at least not anything that Josh could make out.

This was not like her. Why wouldn't she answer?

'Is it dad? Has something happened to him?'

His mother sobbed again but this time she shook her head.

'Dad's okay then?' he said, needing to get a more definite answer.

He put his hand over his mother's and tried to take the crumpled photo from her. After a moment's resistance her hand uncurled and he was drawing the twisted scrap away until he could unfurl it. It was a crushed picture of Josh and Gary. It had been taken that year when they had gone to the beach for a summer holiday,

It was the best holiday Josh ever remembered because it was before Gary thought Josh was too young to have fun with. He still included him in his games and Josh doted on his older brother's every word.

'Gary?' Josh's heart sank. Gary again, their golden boy, why didn't something in his life not have to do with Gary?

But this was more than usual. His heart started thumping. 'Mum what's happened to Gary? Mum? Mum, tell me!' Josh's voice got louder and louder until it was almost a shriek.

He and Gary had had their differences in the last few years before he left but they had still been close and eventually after Gary had been away for months Josh found it was easier to convince himself that Gary was away having a great time with his mates while Josh was having to put up with his parents going loco.

'Mum!' He shook his mum's arm. 'Tell me. What's happened? Is it Gary?'

She looked up at Josh her eyes red and weary. Josh wasn't sure he wanted to hear what she had to say.

'Tell me, Mum. What is it?' He shook her again, more gently this time.

'A-a body.' The word was more of a groan. 'They've found a body.' She shrugged slowly, as if even that was hard work, and sat shaking her head from side to side. 'They don't know for sure. It-it was in the sea, for a long time.'

Josh shuddered. 'It can't be Gary, Mum. Can it?'

He slumped down beside his mother, trying not to think about it, but horrific visions of bloated bodies covered in slime washing up on the shore rose in his head like a horror movie. His stomach clenched and his mouth began to water, sharp and sour. Josh rushed to the bathroom and just made it before the vomit bubbled up and took control, acidic and scalding in his throat.

When his father came home late that night his eyes were rimmed with red, which could have been lack of sleep, Josh wasn't sure. The police had said it might take a bit of time to get any kind of identification from the body because it had been in the water for so long. It had probably been stuck in a deep ridge beneath the surface but the recent strong winds and high tides meant that the body had been washed up and hidden between rocks until a local fisherman found it. The police were going to try and identify it by the dental records.

All the next day they wandered about the house, each doing all the ordinary day to day things as if they were robots, hardly speaking; just waiting for the call. The police had said they would let them know as soon as forensics had managed to establish whether or not it was Gary.

At night Josh had nightmares where he was chased by a large swamp monster with Gary's face, except the face had rotted and been eaten away.

Hollow-eyed, on the third morning, he didn't want to get out of bed or go to school at all. When the phone rang he hid under the covers not wanting to know.

His father's footsteps were a measured tread on the stairs and he heard him come into his room.

'Go away! Don't tell me. I don't want to know!'

His father sat on the bed beside him and stroked his hair gently. 'It's all right, Josh. It wasn't Gary.'

'It wasn't?' He needed a moment or two to let it sink in.

'No. It wasn't him.'

Josh sat up and pulled the covers over his head to hide his tears.

'We still don't know where he is,' his dad said quietly. 'But at least your mother has some hope again.'

His mother? Didn't anyone realise that he was just as upset as his mother? It was his brother, too. He didn't say the words but one look at his dad's face and he knew he understood. At least for the moment they were as close as they had ever been.

Maybe I could use my phone, if I could reach it. It hurts if I move but perhaps I could get it from my pocket if I move very slowly. Yes, that's the edge of it now. Why don't my fingers work properly?

Got it!

Now, as long as I don't drop it. I can hardly feel my hands they are so cold, and my fingers are beginning to feel stiff.

I never really appreciated the fact that my phone lights up when I use it. Even that little bit of light is good. I could call someone, but who would I call? Who would understand or be able to help? It's probably too late, I don't think I have that long.

Mum and Dad will most likely be out anyway. They were going to see that woman from the 'Missing Bureau' or something like that. Apparently there is a new thing where they can put information out and it comes up in other countries and alerts people that someone wants to speak to them.

Mum's been trying to get word out to Gary, wherever he is, to let him know that it is enough if he just lets them know he's okay—still alive, she means, but that is another thing you are not allowed to say in our house.

Gary probably left because he was having a hard time at school and they kept pestering him at home. I think he knew he wasn't going to pass any of his exams and Dad and mum expected so much of him because he'd always been brilliant at school. They were sure he was destined to become some famous scientist or something and were not going to let him waste his life with his silly dreams of being a popstar, they said. But for Gary it was so much more than that and they just didn't understand.

Gary told me once that all he wanted to do was play in a band but he knew mum and dad would never let him do that. Mum thought all bands did was get high and make trouble. Gary tried to tell her about the music but she wouldn't even let him begin to discuss it. She started talking over him and saying how stupid it was because he could be a scientist or a lawyer, or something she approved of and dad just got angry with him.

I wasn't much help but I could have told them. Listening to him playing his guitar made the hairs stand up at the back of my neck. I knew he was good, but I was only his little brother and no one listened to me anyway. Not that much has changed, even now.

I suppose I could call Skye, but she's probably at that chess club she goes to and I don't think she would speak to me anyway. She was so furious when she realised I had been the one who'd stabbed Ranj. She never even waited to hear what had happened.

I think my phone is about to run out of charge, I can see the light flickering, it won't last long now. There it goes, just one last solitary beep! It's a bit like me, alone and running out of power as the blood drains away into the snow.

I can't even call anyone now.

Why didn't I do it when there was some charge left?

I really want to speak to someone...anyone.

I don't want to be alone anymore.

The blood is all over the place now. The snow is deeper, hiding some of it. I wonder if the snow will get thick enough to cover me up completely? Or will it just turn to rain and wash the snow away. Will it wash away the blood, and me with it?

Why did I end up like this? It's not fair, I want to go home.

I didn't mean it to happen, any of it, I just want to go home.

Does nobody care where I am?

Why won't anyone come and look for me?

NINE: Why?

Sunday evening

His mother had insisted that he put on his smart trousers and shirt to visit Ranj in the hospital. Josh had wanted to wear his jeans but she had made such a thing about it he caved and let her have her own way. He wasn't up to having a real blast off with his mum, he had too much on his mind.

When they reached the ward the nurse showed them into a curtained-off area at the end. There was Ranj, all hooked up to wires and looking thin and insignificant, dwarfed by the machines around his bed. Ranj's mother was there waiting but Josh couldn't meet her eyes even when she smiled at him.

Ranj was trying to open his eyes but they seemed to be almost too heavy.

'It's the painkillers,' his mother explained. 'They make him sleepy, but at least they keep the pain away. They say he's past the worst now.' She put her hand on Josh's arm. 'He's been asking about you almost non stop. I know he wants to speak to you, but you can't stay too long, he gets very tired.'

Josh swallowed. This was the hardest thing he had ever done. Ranj was lying there, almost dying because of what he had done. Judging by how his mother was acting Ranj had not told his mum anything about what had happened.

Feeling his mother's hand on his back gently pushing him forward, Josh stepped towards the bed as if he was approaching a wild animal that would jump up and devour him at any given moment.

'Go on.' His mother urged him forward again. 'You sit by the bed and speak to him while Ranj's mum and I go and get a cup of tea.'

Sitting on the edge of the chair as if poised for flight, Josh waited until their mothers had left.

'Ranj?' he whispered, scared to raise his voice and finding himself suddenly breathless. 'Ranj? It's me, Josh.' Looking around to make sure they were alone he turned back to the bed. 'I'm sorr–'

Ranj's eyes flipped open and they seemed out of focus for a moment then they flashed and Josh thought he could see a burning anger in them, like a surge of hate and accusation. 'Why?'

The word was barely more than a whisper but it cut through Josh more painfully than the sharpest knife.

Josh stood up and without another glance at Ranj, he ran. He didn't stop running until he was outside in the rain. Not sure where to go he just kept running on and on, oblivious to the driving rain drenching his shirt, the cold that seeped through the thin material or the puddles that splashed around his feet; soaking through his shoes and splashing mud up across his pale grey trousers making them heavy and wet, dragging around his legs.

All he could think about was that accusing look and the single word.

Why?

Why had he done it? Why had he gone to the hospital? Why had he stopped being mates with Ranj? Why had he left him to become one of Harry's gang when he knew that all Ranj had wanted was to be with Josh; to be his best mate as he had always been?

Why had he taken his knife with him at all?

Why had he almost killed his oldest friend?

Why?

As he ran he felt as if that moment was happening again and again, as it had replayed in his head every hour of the day and all during the night, for the last 24 hours.

He could feel the blade's resistance to Ranj's clothes and then the soft sickening slither as it slid into his body and the heat of the blood as it flowed over Josh's hand. Ranj's blood—his best mate who had trusted him until Josh let him down so badly.

The road under his feet had turned to grass but Josh didn't notice. He didn't care where he was and as his feet got heavy, encrusted with thick mud, his legs took him forward automatically, running him towards the harder ground. But his thoughts were still left behind, beside the bed. In his head he was still staring at Ranj, held captive by that accusing stare, that hurt look he couldn't bear. Even with his eyes closed he could see it. He couldn't run fast enough or far enough because that look was following him.

It was only when he finally reached the edge of the motorway that Josh stopped. He stared at the cars flying past at speed knowing that he couldn't get beyond them easily. Unable to make a decision and suddenly drained of all energy, his feet stopped.

The rain was dripping down his face and plastering his wet hair into his eyes as he faced the blurring flash of cars; roaring as they thundered by on the road in front of him. He had been running so hard the air he was gulping into his lungs burnt its way down his throat.

His brain refused to decide what to do next. A great weariness came over him and he sank to the ground not caring if it was wet or muddy or that the cars streaking past were showering him with freezing cold water.

There was a cry behind him, but he didn't hear it beyond a subconscious awareness that it was getting louder. A kind of shrieking call that repeated again and again like some frantic wild bird, until it finally cut through the thick curtain of despair and formed into a word.

A single, familiar word.

His name.

'Josh! Josh!' His mother's voice was hoarse from shouting and breathless from running, her footsteps thudding through the wet grass as they came closer and closer.

'Josh!'

All of a sudden people, questions and hands surrounded him. None of it made sense to him but he didn't care. Someone threw a coat over his shoulders and it deflected the rain but made the cold wetness of his clothes feel like ice against his already frozen skin.

Later he could never remember what had happened next. The shocking moment when the cold wind and rain stopped and the warmth of the car around him merged in memory with standing in his bedroom, his dad trying to strip off wet clothes that the rain had cemented to his cold, wet skin. His mum drying his wet skin with a warm towel, and then he was in bed, asleep in a world of frantic dreams.

When he eventually woke up Josh had no idea what time it was. It was dark, but it got dark early at this time of year. His hand reached for the bedside lamp but he stopped. Would that bring his parents in? He couldn't face speaking to anyone.

Using what little light there was in the room he squinted at the clock but he couldn't see it and he had no idea whether it was night or morning.

As he lay trying to make some sense of what had happened, Ranj's face appeared in the back of his head, his eyes accusing, and Josh could hear him ask again and again. 'Why?'

The knife fight came back to him as clearly as watching a film.

He had been with Danny, messing about because it was Sunday morning and they were planning to go and see what was happening at the parade later in the day.

Danny had been complaining that Harry and the YHT had been taunting him about Josh on Friday at school, but Josh had assumed it was just the normal everyday routine with the YHT. He'd missed it all because he had been in detention and forced to stay in the classroom for the school lunch break and he was fairly sure that Danny had exaggerated it all.

Harry was waiting to get back at Josh because of Sandie telling him to crawl under a rock and stay there, in front of the entire year. Harry said it was all Josh's fault and swore he would get even with him.

Josh knew that it was just an excuse. Josh and Harry had been enemies for as long as Josh could remember. Harry pretty much ruled their year. He was bigger than most of them and made sure no one crossed him, but for some reason he seemed to find Josh his greatest challenge. Josh wondered if it was because every now and then he stood up to Harry, precious few others ever did.

He sometimes wished he could keep his mouth shut; it would stop him getting into quite so much trouble, but there was something about Harry that made him angry and before he knew it he'd shot his mouth off again. Several times it had descended into a fist fight, but in the last while Harry and the YHT had started carrying knives and it all seemed to have notched up a level.

So Josh had taken to carrying a knife too, Gary's knife, just in case.

He and Danny were heading into town that morning and Josh was only paying a little attention to what Danny was saying; he was busy thinking about something Skye had said to him online the day before. She had been talking about some new game she had been given as a present, and wanted to challenge him to a race to the death. He'd sent her a text to say he was up for it and laughed at her response. He was concentrating on his phone, holding it up to show Danny what she'd said in her text.

That was why Danny's first cry of surprise had gone almost unnoticed. The lane was wider at the top end but further down it narrowed sharply, barely leaving room to walk side by side. They had just reached that point when Danny shouted at him.

'Josh!'

Josh looked up and saw Harry in front of him with Ranj and Syd. He spun around to see that two others had come up behind, blocking them in. They had walked into a trap.

Danny started making a low groaning noise that Josh hated. 'Shut it, Danny!' he snapped, trying to think of a way out.

Harry swaggered, stretching out his arm towards Josh and flicking his wrist. 'Payback time!' He had a grin on his face that boded badly for the two of them.

The winter sun was struggling to warm the morning and it was quite murky in the lane because of all the trees that had grown up behind the narrow walls. The pale sunlight caught on the blade of the long knife in Harry's hand.

Josh reached into his back pocket and drew his own, much shorter, knife. He carried it for show really, and to ward off trouble, but he never thought he would have to use it. The two YHT behind him filled the narrow space in the alleyway so that they had nowhere to run.

Ranj looked unhappy but Harry and Syd were eager for a fight to start.

'What's up, Harry?' Josh deliberately made his voice mocking and light, but he wasn't sure how long he could keep it steady. Nerves were already getting the better of him and his knee seemed to have developed a life of its own, wanting to shake and shudder for no reason. 'Not found any small people to torture today?'

'I found you, Josh. Who else do I need?' With his knife hand he lunged at Josh, who just managed to dance out of the way in time to avoid a cut.

'Harry!' Ranj sounded scared. 'You said no one was going to get hurt!'

Josh wondered if Ranj was playing for time. Josh knew he was never happy about any of them carrying knives.

'Did I?' Harry jeered at Ranj, 'Now, why would I have said a thing like that? Anyone else hear me say that?'

Syd laughed with him, an unpleasant sound, and threw a disparaging look at Ranj but he stayed well behind him, using Ranj as a shield.

Harry stepped closer, and Josh could sense that the two boys behind him were moving in, forcing him and Danny forwards, towards Harry who was holding his knife threateningly close to Josh.

'Just one jab and you're dogmeat, Josh. Let's rearrange those pretty boy looks of yours. Give me a good reason why I shouldn't just slice you up here and now.' Harry waved the knife around towards Josh's face. Josh knew he was just playing with him; it was a test of nerves.

'Because you've not got the nerve, Harry. But maybe I have. What do you think?' Josh faced him up and held up his knife, feeling his palms sweating as he gripped the knife tighter, his knuckles showing white under the skin. Harry was taller and heavier but Josh held his gaze, as if capturing him, willing him not to move. While he stared into Harry's hard blue eyes he was watching his opponent's knife hand at the very edge of his vision.

His mind was racing, looking for opportunities to get out of the situation in one piece. With a shock Josh realised that Harry wasn't bluffing, he meant to use the knife. But Josh was still trying to believe that it was actually happening. He had been sure that Harry wouldn't really do it, but now he wasn't so sure.

'Let's see who's chicken then?' Harry leaned forward towards Josh but just at that moment Ranj pushed past Harry and got between them.

'Wait!' he shouted, but it was already too late.

Josh had just raised his knife to defend himself when Harry grabbed Ranj and pushed him towards Josh.

Josh could feel the rough cloth of Ranj's jacket against the back of his hand. His knife felt heavy as Ranj fell against him, the blade buried deep inside him.

Looking up, Josh saw the surprised look on Ranj's face and behind him Harry was grinning. That was what Josh had remembered when he and Danny were on the swings. Harry had looked so pleased with himself. Josh realised he and Ranj had been played. They had done exactly what Harry wanted.

TEN: Birthday Blues

Monday morning

There was smoke, a lot of smoke. Black, thick and choking. Skye's eyes were streaming and when she put her hand up to her face it came away covered in skin and blood. She could do nothing to stop it. It was happening again.

'Help me, help me, MUMMY!' Her high five-year-old voice wailed, as the nightmare ran its course.

She groaned and tossed in her sleep, the familiar nightmare stealing her slumber, leaving her trembling and wide awake. It was such a long time ago but it was as clear and real as if it had been only last week.

She remembered that it was a quiet, warm and sunny day, the kind of day you long for in the summer. All the week before the weather had been cold and rainy, but today was special and it was sunny, so everything was perfect.

Skye could hear the other children playing in the park and although she was only five years old for once she didn't mind that she wasn't able to run and join them. This was a special day and it felt like she had waited for a very long time for it to arrive. There was a sense of excitement in the air and her mum had been singing all morning, in that tuneless way she had. It was a sound that said everything was right with the world, she was safe and loved and her mum was happy.

She walked down the hall and stopped beside the grandfather clock, watching the pendulum swinging back and forth, back and forth. She was mesmerised by it, intrigued by the way it never stopped. It had been her grandfather's clock and her Gran told her that she wound it up every day at the same time, just as her granddad used to do every day until the day he died. Gran said she intended to do the same until the Good Lord came for her.

Skye had wondered what she meant but when she looked worried and asked when He was coming, her grandmother just smiled and gave her a big hug. 'Not for a long while, I hope. Not for a long while yet.'

Impatiently watching out of the narrow hall window, she hoped her Gran wouldn't be too much longer, but she walked quite slowly and the cemetery was a long walk away. Skye knew that because once Gran had taken her along, to put flowers on her granddad's grave. When they walked back home it seemed so far that Skye thought they might never reach home again.

She ran back into the kitchen. 'Is it time, yet, Mum?' she asked for the hundredth time that morning, and for the hundredth time her mum said, 'Not yet, Skye, but it won't be long now.'

She had never been good at waiting.

'Why don't you go out and wait by the front step,' her mum suggested, seeing how impatient she was. 'Just stay on the step, mind, don't wander off and don't go onto the road.'

'I won't mummy,' Skye had promised.

She ran back and sat down on the front step. It was her birthday today, and as soon as her Gran got home they were all going out for a special birthday treat. She couldn't wait.

'You are such a big girl,' her mum had said, 'so for your birthday we are going to go to the stables that your Uncle Jack runs and you can go on a pony ride!'

'He's not really your uncle, just a friend of Mummy's,' her Gran had told her. 'But he's a good man,' she added with a little smile. 'Afterwards we are going out for tea and you can have cakes and ice cream and anything you want as a special treat.'

Skye was so excited. She loved horses and she wanted to have some of her own one day, just like 'uncle' Jimmy.

She had taken her toy horse out to the front step with her so that she could play with it while she was keeping one eye on the road to see if her Gran was coming. It seemed to take forever but then she spotted her Gran walking back across the park. Skye knew she wasn't allowed to leave the step but she wished she could run to meet her.

She stood up, shouting and waving. In her excitement she stepped down onto the second step and then the next, until she was down on the pavement. She waved to her Gran and walked a couple of steps away from the house, still staying on the pavement, because she knew it wasn't safe to cross the road by herself.

She wished Gran would hurry up.

She took another step along the pavement just a little bit away from the house. It wasn't far and Gran was almost at the edge of the road.

'Hurry up, Gran!' she shouted, jumping up and down with all of her five year old enthusiasm.

'Now you stay where you are until I get across this road,' her Gran called to her, looking a little worried. 'Wait there for me!' But Skye knew she had to wait and she stayed away from the road's edge.

Her Gran stepped out onto the road.

The blast threw Skye to the ground and tossed her toy horse onto the pavement just out of the reach of her hand. No one could hear her young screams above the noise of the explosion and the rumble of falling masonry. Clouds of thick smoke and dust filled the air and somewhere in the midst of it she heard her Gran shrieking her name.

A second explosion, louder than the first, blew out the windows all along the street sending a cascade of shattered glass onto the pavements. Skye curled into a tight ball and screamed again as it rained down on her and a third explosion rocked the street, again. A huge block of stone crashed onto the pavement inches from her head, crushing her toy horse and showering her with chips of stone and dust. She screamed until her voice gave way, and the last thing she remembered was looking at the enormous slab of masonry right beside her head, and the smashed body of her precious toy horse crushed beneath it. A terrible pain in her arm made her cry out.

'Help me, Mummy, help me…MUMMY!'

Skye tried to open her eyes but all around her was stone and black dust, choking smoke, loud noises and sudden quiet, blood and fear and a deep hurt that nothing would take away. She shuddered and buried her head in the pillow already damp with tears, searching for the peace of a dreamless sleep and wishing she could forget.

• • •

The first orange hints of morning streaked across the white clouds outside his window and Josh realised he must have fallen asleep again. The display on his clock proved it, showing 7.30am, so it was obviously morning. He stretched languorously, enjoying the warmth of his bed, but when he pictured Ranj in the hospital it robbed him of that moment's contentment and he didn't want to stay in bed any longer.

Switching on his computer he hoped Skye would be up. He knew she was usually up early.

SPIKE writes
u up?

WILDCAT writes
Morning early bird. u okay? I heard things were bad yesterday.

SPIKE writes
How do u find out everything?

WILDCAT writes
My mum spoke to ur's last night

SPIKE writes
No secrets in the world r there?

WILDCAT writes
Suppose not, do u need secrets?

SPIKE writes
Everyone needs secrets…

WILDCAT writes
Interesting!!!! Is that why u can't sleep?

SPIKE writes
i was thinking bout Ranj

WILDCAT writes
I saw him last night

SPIKE writes
He say anything?

WILDCAT writes
Not much he askd if I knew if u were ok.

SPIKE writes
He hates me.

WILDCAT writes
don't think so.

SPIKE writes
u shd have seen the way he lookd at me

WILDCAT writes
Is that what happened? he sd u just got up and ran off. thot U'd been forced 2 come and see him.

SPIKE writes
He tell U what happened?

WILDCAT writes
sd U'd tell me.

SPIKE writes
Why?

WILDCAT writes
don't know. U don't have 2

SPIKE writes
Can U tell him i'm sorry—bout what happened.

WILDCAT writes
tell him Ur self.

WILDCAT writes
…well?

SPIKE writes
can't.

WILDCAT writes
course U can. U just open Ur mouth and think the words and they come out all by themselves.

SPIKE writes
No, can't go back there.

WILDCAT writes
Time 2 stop thinking bout Ur self. He wanted 2 see U, remember.

SPIKE writes
2 tell me he hates me.

WILDCAT writes
No, he doesn't. Do U want Me 2 come with U?

SPIKE writes

Would U do that?

WILDCAT writes
Yup, all U had 2 do was ask.

SPIKE writes
don't know if my parents will let me go.

WILDCAT writes
Tell them U want 2 go back 2 the hospital and Ranj sd he wanted 2 see you again.

SPIKE writes
OK, might just work.

WILDCAT writes
I'll come over after breakfast if you like. 2 help persuade the parents!

Skye turned off her computer and got ready for school. Eating breakfast she could see Gran wanted to say something about last night. Gran knew she'd been having nightmares again; she'd probably been woken up by Skye's cries. She used to come in and try to comfort her but Skye hated the sad look in her eyes, it made her feel worse rather than better. Gran just sat there and looked at her, sadly. Skye hoped she wouldn't start that conversation. They'd had it so many times and she wasn't in the mood this morning.

'See you later, Gran,' she said, grabbing her bag and pulling her sleeve down to cover her hand before opening the door and setting off for school. 'I won't be late.'

She saw her Gran bite her lip on the question that she now knew better than to ask; knowing her answer would be the same as it had always been.

Skye didn't want to remember her birthday. She refused to open birthday cards and threw a tantrum at the thought of any kind of celebration.

There was nothing to celebrate. It had been the day the gas cooker exploded taking their whole house with it, the day she had lost her mother, the day that had marked her forever mentally and physically. A day of so much promise that had become a constant nightmare of memories she could never forget. Why would she want to celebrate it? What was so special about getting a year older, it happened to everyone, every year.

She slammed the door on her way out, and then felt bad about it. She wasn't often angry but today was the one day in the year she felt she had every right to be angry. At least she was going to walk to school with Josh, thinking about that made her smile, chasing away the anger.

Josh headed to the shower, it was just after 8 am. He slipped downstairs quietly as soon as he was dressed, started the kettle boiling and put on some toast.

'You slept well, then?' His dad came into the kitchen behind him, making him jump at the sound of his voice.

'Sorry, Dad I didn't hear you come in, I was miles away.'

His dad was watching him with a strange look on his face. 'We need to talk, Josh.'

'I know, Dad, but can we do it later? I've got to get to school.' He looked as if he was about to argue with him when his mother came in.

'Mum, I want to go back to the hospital this afternoon. Skye said she's going in, can I go with her? She said Ranj asked her to tell me to come back and see him again.'

His parents exchanged glances and then his mother nodded. 'Are you sure you want to this time?'

'Yes, I really do. I'm sorry about yesterday. It was all just a bit too much.'

He could tell his parents desperately wanted to ask him what it was all about but luckily the phone rang. His mother went off to answer it and Josh took his toast upstairs to his room. He knew his father wouldn't come up when his mum wasn't around; tackling him together was their style, when dad was at home at least. And his mum never had short conversations on the phone so he was safe from their questions for a bit. He just hoped that Skye would arrive soon.

The doorbell rang.

'I'll get it.' Josh breezed down the stairs breathing a huge sigh of relief when he saw it was Skye. She followed him into the kitchen and he was amused at the way his dad never seemed to know how to speak to her. He mumbled something and left the room.

A few moments later his mum came back into the kitchen. 'Hello Skye. Josh tells me you are going into the hospital this afternoon?'

Skye nodded. 'I've a free afternoon. Ranj said he wanted to see Josh and I said I'd go in with him.'

Josh saw his mum thinking about it. 'That was the police, again, Josh,' she told him. 'They want to interview you. Do you think you will be feeling up to it this afternoon, after you come back from the hospital, of course? They're coming here around 4pm.'

'Suppose so.' Josh felt his stomach clench at the thought, but he reassured himself that by then he would have heard what Ranj had told the police. Josh could just make his story the same.

'It was that nice policewoman I spoke to yesterday,' his mother was saying. 'She says she's happy to come here. It'll be better than going to the police station, won't it?'

Josh turned to Skye 'We'd better go or we'll be late.'

His dad met them in the hall. 'I'll give you a lift to the hospital in the car this afternoon. I'll pick you up from school.' Josh saw his mum give a slight nod of approval.

'It's okay, Dad, really.' Josh knew his parents didn't want him to disappear, at least until the police had been to talk to him.

'I think your dad should take you. Anyway it's raining and quite cold out. And you need to be back in time for the policewoman coming this afternoon, anyway.'

'That will be great, thanks,' Skye said, grinning at his dad and Josh rolled his eyes. He realised they weren't going to let them go without one of his parents but she didn't have to agree so happily.

'I'll call the school and let them know we'll be picking you up at lunchtime.'

As they left the house Josh heard his mother speaking to the school, telling them that he had to go to the hospital. He thought his mother was being less than truthful because the way she said it made it sound as if Josh was attending hospital not that he was just visiting. But he realised his mother wouldn't want to say he had to speak to the police afterwards, that would be too embarrassing.

I never thought it would be like this.

It is so easy to have a knife in your hand, feeling so strong and protected by that single piece of sharp steel. The feeling that just brandishing it at someone was going to make them think twice, or even run away.

I used to have all these ideas; they seem stupid now.

Things like how you had control of everything when you had a knife in your hand.

Did I really think that someone like Harry would stop and listen to what I said and wouldn't fight me because I had a knife, just like him?

Did I really think having a knife meant that I could face him off, or he would be scared of me because I drew a knife?

To be honest it just felt good, like I had power because of the knife.

How stupid was that? Look at me now!

It wasn't something I really thought about in so many words, it was more of a feeling, a sense of all that, of all the emotions whirling around my gut.

But I never thought about what it would feel like to be on the other side of the knife.

I never thought about what it would be like, what it would feel like when I thought I had killed Ranj.

I didn't like it. Not one bit.

If I ever thought about what would happen if I died it was more like how much people would miss me and what they would say about me when I was gone. Stupid really, I know that now, because I won't be there to find out, will I?

I never realised how much it would hurt, how scary it would be. I never considered the important things like the simple fact that—I don't want to be DEAD!

I really don't want to die, not yet. I'm not ready. There are things I want to do. And it didn't hurt at first but now it hurts—a lot.

And there's Skye.

I really like her but I never told her that. I kind of wish I had now, but she would probably have laughed. I was more worried what people like Harry would say if he found out. He would have sneered and made some comment about her hand and my having a nerdy girlfriend.

Why was I so worried about what he thought? Why didn't I see that he was such a loser, and if I cared about things like that it just meant that I was turning into someone just like him.

A loser.

That's what I will be in a few minutes anyway.

A loser.

A dead loser.

ELEVEN: In the News

Monday morning

School was buzzing with the news about Ranj getting stabbed and outside the school gates was a mass of photographers from all the newspapers and even a TV crew with their huge cameras and furry boom microphones. But the teachers were out, on the lookout, stopping the Press from talking to anyone.

At assembly it was a totally agitated Head Teacher who addressed the whole school.

'We are helping the police with their enquiries and they may want to interview some of you. No one is to speak to any member of the Press. We are contacting your parents, but if anyone has any information please come and speak to either myself, or one of the teachers. We will not tolerate this kind of behaviour by any pupil in our school and it is for your own safety that we need to find the culprit.'

He told the school that Ranj was recovering in hospital but everyone seemed to know that already. Josh caught sight of Harry and Syd across the hall. Syd made an obscene gesture and Josh turned away quickly. Skye was giving him an encouraging smile but Josh just wanted to get out of there.

All morning other kids kept coming up to

Josh and Danny and asking about Ranj. Josh had warned Danny on their way to school.

'Whatever anyone says, keep schtum and don't tell them anything, Danny. We need to keep this between ourselves.'

'What if the police are there, Josh? I don't want to get into trouble with them. I can't.'

'So we say nothing, to anyone, especially the police. We were at the carnival when we heard about Ranj, that's it.'

At morning break he and Danny were called to see Mr Hatten, the Head Teacher. As they approached his office Harry and Syd came swaggering out. Mr Hatten's secretary was watching so Harry did no more than make a threatening face at Josh, who completely ignored him. Danny snarled back at him but that only earned him a sharp reprimand from the secretary who ushered them both into her office to wait to be called.

Mr Hatten was busy writing something when Josh entered his room. He barely looked up but signalled towards one of the two seats opposite the desk and continued writing.

Josh wasn't sure what to do and squirmed a bit in his seat until he noticed that every now and then Mr Hatten's eyes flickered towards him. He realised what Mr Hatten was doing, he was making Josh sit for a while, making him wait to put him on edge.

Even knowing that didn't help. Josh was on edge.

He tried not to fidget but it was almost impossible. He wasn't sure what Mr Hatten knew but at least he knew that Harry wouldn't have said anything. He wouldn't grass anyone up to the Head; he despised Hatten almost as much as he hated the police.

Finally Mr Hatten looked up and carefully put the top on his fountain pen. He was finicky about things like that, everything about him was precise and neat, even his hair, which he carefully combed across his head like bits of string in an attempt to hide his bald patch, much to the amusement of his pupils.

'Well, Josh. Want to tell me anything about what happened to Ranj? You and he used to be really close pals, didn't you?'

Josh stared at his feet, suddenly fascinated by the single thread that had come frayed from the laces of his trainers and was curled in a spiral like a piece of silver wire.

'Josh?'

Josh shrugged and kept looking down.

'If you can tell me anything, we can try to stop this kind of thing happening again. You wouldn't like this to happen to you, would you? I am sure you must have heard something?'

Josh shook his head.

'Don't you want us to find out who did it?'

Josh didn't move a muscle. The silence stretched until he was sure Mr Hatten knew something he wasn't saying. Josh felt himself about to panic when he heard the Head take a deep breath. He picked up his pen, again. 'If you find there is something you want to tell me, my door is always open, Josh.'

Realising that this was his signal to leave, Josh made his escape. He opened the door and saw Danny sitting there opposite the secretary, looking really nervous.

'Josh!' Mr Hatten called to him before he closed the door.

Josh looked back at him, meeting his eyes for the first time. He tried not to breathe as he returned Mr Hatten's stare.

'Remember that Ranj is your friend. He will be relying on you to be a good friend to him now and tell anything you know about what happened yesterday, so that we can catch the person who did it and stop them hurting someone else.' He paused with a meaningful look. Josh thought in any other circumstance he would have laughed his head off about that look, but he didn't feel like laughing.

'You can ask Danny to come in now.'

Josh nodded quickly and stared hard at Danny as he went into the Head's room, a look that said 'Say nothing!'

Danny closed the door behind him just as the end of break bell sounded.

Josh didn't get another chance to speak to Danny. They had different classes before lunch and his father arrived to collect him and Skye as soon as the lunch break started. The hospital was just a short drive away but they all sat silently in the car, which suited Josh. Skye looked out of the window while Josh was almost mesmerised by the rain on the windscreen and the swish swash of the wipers as they struggled to keep the screen clear. He didn't know what to say to his father that wouldn't make things more complicated, and worse still what was he going to say to the police? Mr Hatten had been bad enough this morning at school.

He was sure that once he'd had a chance to speak to Ranj, to find out what he'd told the police, it would be it easier to construct a believable story. Josh never had problems making adults believe him; he just widened his eyes and looked worried, that usually worked.

Another problem was beginning to bother him. What would Skye say if she found out that he'd been the one who had stabbed Ranj? There were too many things going around in his head to start to worry about that. He'd deal with that when the time came. He wasn't about to tell her and maybe she'd never find out.

TWELVE: Wanted

Monday morning

Ranj lay in his bed in the hospital and thought about what had happened the night before, when Josh came in to see him. He'd been over it in his head again and again ever since it happened. He had wanted to speak to Josh but when he woke up and saw Josh looking down at him something inside turned sour. All he could think about was the way Josh had stopped speaking to him those months before, and had taken up with Danny. Ranj felt betrayed. He and Josh had been really tight, they did everything together, even when Josh's brother disappeared. Even then it was Ranj that Josh rushed to see, to tell him about it. When had things changed?

Seeing Josh looking all cocky and sure of himself had made Ranj angry. Not really angry with Josh, but with everything that had happened and the way it had happened. He just wanted things to be the way they used to be, him and Josh—best mates.

He'd been really surprised when Josh ran out of the ward. He told Skye when she came in later that he was hoping Josh would come back in to see him again, so that they could talk.

• • •

Josh's mobile went off as his dad parked the car in the hospital car park.

'Josh! Where are you?'

'Danny? What's up?'

'I've got to see you. Something's happened.'

'What is it, Danny? I can't talk just now we're about to go into the hospital to see Ranj. Can't it wait?'

'No. It can't. I'm coming over there. Where will you be? We have to talk, now!'

Josh couldn't imagine what on earth was wrong with Danny. He was never this insistent.

'Ward 15. We're going in now, Skye's with me, and my dad.'

'I won't be long. We have to talk. Alone!'

Josh knew how much his father hated hospitals and he was just trying to persuade him that he didn't need to come in with them because Ranj wasn't allowed more than two visitors at a time, when his father's mobile went off.

'Okay, Josh, I'll take this in the car and wait for you here.'

When they got to the ward Skye went in first, Josh still wasn't sure if he could manage it at all. He peered over Skye's shoulder and was relieved when Ranj looked at him not exactly smiling but at least he wasn't scowling.

'Hi, Ranj.' Josh wished he could be as casual as Skye, the way he and Ranj used to be, but there was too much between them now, too much distrust and too many problems. Ranj was sitting up in bed and looking much better after a night's sleep.

'Hello, Josh.'

He still looked pale but Josh didn't see that particular look in his eyes that had made him run off the night before. He was desperate to ask him what he had told the police but he didn't know how to start, and Skye was there. He had no idea how she would react if she found out.

Ranj had been thinking the same thing. 'Skye, any chance you could go and get me some chocolate from the hospital shop?'

Skye went off immediately, glad to have an excuse to leave the boys alone. She could see they needed to talk without anyone else there and she'd done her bit in getting Josh to the hospital. Josh hadn't bolted out of the door yet, so it looked like they would be fine.

'Ranj, I'm sorry, really.' Josh stumbled over the words and then clenched his teeth in the silence that followed. He waited, unable to say another word.

Ranj felt in control and that was a strange feeling when it came to Josh. He was a little reluctant to spoil the moment, he was enjoying it too much and it wasn't likely to last. 'I didn't tell the police anything, you know,' he said, after a pause that was about as long as he could manage.

'You didn't?' Josh felt as if all his muscles had

been tensed up and suddenly they were released all at once.

'What was I going to say to them? Harry would kill me if I welched on him and I wasn't going to say it was you, was I?'

'But...' Josh couldn't bring himself to say the words that were ringing in his head. *It was me; I did it.*

'Anyway, I thought you should know, because I think they want to speak to you. Someone has said something to them about you being there. They seemed to know that already, but I wanted you to know it wasn't me. I never told them. You know I wouldn't.'

Josh had no answer to that.

With the important stuff out of the way, he and Ranj spoke for a bit, neither of them wanting to say anything particular, so it was with a sense of relief that Josh noticed Skye returning with the chocolate.

A few moments later the door of the ward burst open and Danny rushed in. A few of the other visiting relatives looked up and the nurse glared at him, but he didn't leave the nurses' station when Danny slowed down and started to walk more calmly towards the bed.

'Josh, we've g-g-got to get out of here!' His breathless whisper made it sound all the more urgent.

All three of them stared at him.

'What's wrong, Danny?'

Danny looked at Ranj and then at Skye, unsure if he should speak in front of her. Skye raised an eyebrow. 'What is it, Danny? You can tell us, whatever it is. Is it something to do with Ranj getting hurt?'

Danny looked pleadingly at Josh but he just shrugged as if he wasn't bothered what Danny said or who was listening. Josh was exhausted. He didn't know what to feel or do and he felt as if he just didn't care any more, there were too many secrets. The police were waiting for him when he got home and before coming to the hospital he had resigned himself to Ranj having told the police that he'd done it. Now he didn't know what to think.

Danny spoke in a whisper, checking that there was no one close enough to overhear him.

'I overheard Syd talking to some of the YHT. He was b-b-boasting about how he'd called the police anonymously and told them you'd stabbed Ranj and that I'd helped to s-s-set it up.'

Skye heard Josh's sharp intake of breath and watched as he sank into the chair, looking weary. 'It's okay, Josh, You can just tell them it wasn't you. Ranj and Danny will back you up, won't you? Ranj?'

Ranj turned his head away from her and said nothing and Danny was suddenly engrossed in pulling threads from a rip in his jeans. She looked from one to the other in confusion. 'Ranj? Josh? What's going on? You can just tell them. It's that simple.'

Josh buried his head in his hands.

Skye stared at him. She couldn't understand what was wrong.

'No!' It was ridiculous but the question that had entered her head was clamouring to be asked. 'It wasn't you, Josh…was it?'

He didn't answer, but the look on his face was all the answer she needed.

'How could you?'

'That's not how it happened. It was Harry's f-f-fault,' Danny started trying to speak really fast, to make Skye understand. 'He wanted it to happen. H-h-he planned it, and he wanted J-J-Josh to take the blame.'

Skye turned away from the bed, her face like stone. She wasn't listening and a moment later she walked out of the ward without another word.

Josh was more upset by Skye's reaction than he had been by anything else. The look on her face said she hated him. He wanted to run after her and explain but he knew she wouldn't listen.

'We've got to go.' Danny's voice penetrated his misery.

'Where?'

'I don't know. Away, anywh-wh-where.'

'Why?' Ranj asked him. 'Danny, what's the matter? Skye's got a point. Josh just needs to tell them it was Harry's fault for setting it up, and that it was an accident. I'll tell them that, too.'

'No,' Josh spoke up. He'd made a decision. 'Danny's right. They'll never believe us, no matter what we say about it. I did it and that's the truth.'

'But where will you go?'

Josh looked at Ranj lying on the bed and made an instant choice. 'No, Ranj I don't think we should tell you. That way if anyone asks you won't know anything anyway. It's for the best. Come on, Danny, let's go.'

Ranj made a face. Josh was excluding him again in favour of Danny. He knew there was a good reason but he couldn't help feeling annoyed by it.

'I really am sorry, Ranj. You do know that, don't you?'

Ranj gave the barest nod but he was still feeling left out.

In the corridor they headed for the lift but Josh stopped when he remembered that the lift doors opened to the front of the hospital. There was a large glass window that looked straight out onto the car park and his dad was sitting in the car opposite the front doors. He might not see them, but Josh wasn't going to take any chances. He led the way down the corridor towards the sign saying 'stairs'.

'GARY! Is that you, Gary?'

There are all these clouds, or is it mist? I can almost see the last of the hazy sunshine but it's cold sunshine, and I can't stop shivering. I saw a figure in the mist a moment ago. It wasn't really distinct, more like a shadow but I'm sure it was Gary.

'Gary come back, don't go!' I'm shouting, but it comes out like a croak as a pain lances through my side. I'm dizzy and breathless. 'Gary,' I whisper. 'Don't leave me here, please, Gary. Come back!'

It was him! I know it was. Does that mean I'm dead, but that would mean that he must be dead, too? I never believed that Gary was dead. I never have. I can feel it; he's out there, somewhere.

It's Gary's birthday next week. Mum always gets upset on his birthday but this year he will be 19. He was 16 when he left, I can hardly believe it was 3 years ago, it seems much longer but that must be right. I used to think he was great, when he wasn't being mean and keeping me out of his room or shouting at me for touching his things. But most of the time we got on fine, as long as I obeyed his rules. Just like most big brothers, I suppose.

He loved his guitar and I knew better than to ever touch that. It was the most important thing in his life. Mum and dad couldn't see that. For ages they used to have blazing arguments but not long before he left he stopped arguing with them and it looked like he was doing exactly what they wanted, he played like the perfect son. I didn't realise why he was doing it at the time, I was just pleased that they had all stopped shouting and slamming doors.

That was when I started getting into trouble for things. I wasn't as smart as Gary; I was a rebel without a reason. Just because someone said black I would say white, if only to be different, I'm not even sure I knew why I did it but it meant I was always getting into trouble over silly things.

Gary let our parents believe he was studying and doing what they wanted, so that they left him alone to do whatever he liked.

Really smart, really! Wish I had thought of that.

So that day when he disappeared I don't remember much about it, except that he and dad had a blazing row a couple of days before. I remember it so clearly because it hadn't happened for so long. Maybe Gary thought dad would have changed his mind and let him do what he wanted...Music was his life, he said, and Dad just laughed and told him he was being childish.

There were all these things in his room, music magazines and sheet music where he had scribbled songs he'd composed himself.

I wonder where he is now. Did he manage to get away and do what he wanted or did he really die in some ditch somewhere, murdered for his guitar

or what little money he had?
  We're not a family any more, we've not been that
since he left.

THIRTEEN: Running

The stairwell echoed with their footsteps as they ran down as fast as they could. On the ground floor Josh cautiously opened the door a little and peered out. It faced away from the window and wasn't far from Reception. He stopped and held his breath. His father was standing at the reception desk. Letting the door close slowly Josh leaned back against the wall and slid down it until he was sitting on the floor. Danny stood over him.

'What's the matter?'

'Dad's out there with a couple of policemen. They must be going up to the ward. I bet Skye told them we were still up there. We'll have to wait a bit until they've gone.'

The seconds and minutes ticked past as if they were in slow motion. Josh got up and took another look outside.

'They've gone,' he whispered. 'Come on. Follow me and stay close but try not to look as if we're hurrying.'

Josh stepped out of the stairwell and keeping his face turned away he tried to avoid looking at the reception desk as they walked towards the door, but all the time he was waiting for someone to call out his name. They reached the door and Danny pushed it open.

The rain had stopped and the sun had broken

through the clouds. It was streaming through the glass doors and windows but once outside a sharp biting wind hit them. Josh shivered, hoping it wasn't going to start to snow. He shrugged into his leather jacket, thankful for its warmth.

The sight of a police car waiting near the door startled them both until they realised that there was no one in it. Josh walked past quickly and in a few moments they were at the hospital gate.

'Where are we going?' Danny was puffing a bit at the pace Josh had set.

'I don't know yet, I need time to think. We have to get away from the hospital first.'

The police reached the ward quite quickly with Josh's father following behind them. 'That's him,' Josh's father pointed out Ranj's bed.

• • •

Ranj had seen them entering the ward and closing his eyes he feigned sleep, trying to control his breathing so that it was slow and deep. He was relying on the thought that they wouldn't try to wake him and he was beginning to feel sleepy anyway, so it wasn't difficult.

'He's asleep,' the policewoman said, in a quiet voice. 'Do you want to ask the nurse if he's seen the other two?'

Ranj's mind was racing. They had obviously not seen the boys downstairs so they had managed to get away. He didn't want to let them know he was awake. If they thought he was asleep they wouldn't ask him questions and at least that way he wouldn't have to say anything.

'Did you see a boy and a girl who were visiting that patient over there?' the policeman asked.

Ranj opened his eyes just enough to see through his lashes. He strained to hear the reply.

'Yes, they were there just a few minutes ago and another boy joined them, but I was called away and I didn't see them leave. They can't have been gone very long. I was only away for a few minutes. I was about to go and speak to them myself. Ranj really needs to rest and he's had quite a few visitors today.'

'We were wanting to ask him a few questions, but he seems to be asleep.' The policeman sounded as if he wanted to wake him up and Ranj held his breath waiting to hear what the nurse would say.

'I'm not surprised he's sleeping, the painkillers will make him sleep for a while. If you want to speak to him it will have to wait until later this evening, I'm afraid.' The nurse led them back to the door of the ward.

Ranj relaxed as he saw them leave and within moments the medicines in his system took effect and he was drifting into a deep sleep.

• • •

'We can go to the park,' Josh told Danny as they made their way along the High Street. 'There's that old summer house there and no one goes there most of the time.'

Danny was following Josh, more worried than he had admitted. If the police wanted to speak to Josh they would need to speak to him, too and that meant they would get in touch with his mother. She would be so worried if the police came to the house and he didn't want that. If his mother got very upset she had problems breathing, and Danny didn't know what would happen if he wasn't there to help her.

The police might call in the social services and he was sure they would put his mother in a home when they found out how ill she was. Danny didn't know if that was definitely true but he was too scared to ask anyone, just in case it was true.

Although the main part of the park was busy the old summerhouse was in an area that few people used because it was still to be renovated. The grass was covered with weeds and there was a lot of litter and broken benches. The sun rarely managed to penetrate the thick bushes and tall trees so that it was always a dark and dismal area.

The old summerhouse was in a terrible state. The paint was peeling and the wooden roof had holes in it, but at least it was some shelter from the wind and the sleet that had started to fall. Josh shivered as they sat down on the dusty floor, the low walls were some protection and no one would see them from outside. In silence they dwelt on their situation, Josh was trying to think of somewhere they could go that the police wouldn't find them, and Danny was worrying about his mother.

I never realised how much Danny had to do at home. It wasn't until he started talking about it, when we were sitting in the summerhouse waiting for it to get dark, that I realised I'd never really asked him or maybe I'd just not listened to him all that much. I thought he was a bit thick because he didn't say much and was always running off home. He started telling me that he was worried about his mum if he didn't get home in time.

'I thought it might be that your dad would beat you up or something. You never mention your dad.'

Danny just stared at me as if I was loony or something. 'My dad's dead. He died years ago when I was little. Some kind of cancer I think. I don't remember him much at all.'

'So what is it then? Why are you always in such a rush to get home?' I fished about in my pocket for the chocolate that Ranj had got from Skye. He'd given it to me saying he wasn't allowed to eat it and we'd need it more than him.

I unwrapped the chocolate bar and broke a chunk off for Danny and one for me. I savoured the smooth sweetness, realising that I had hardly eaten anything since early morning.

Danny took his time chewing it as he spoke. 'It's my mum. She's ill.'

'What's wrong with her?'

'She's almost totally blind and she has problems walking and at times with her breathing as well. She can't do much for herself, really.'

'So? Is there no one else to help her?'

Danny gave a small, bemused laugh. I thought he looked just like a little fat mouse, nibbling on the chocolate with his hair falling into his eyes and his glasses sitting almost at the end of his nose.

'Who? We don't have any relatives. Mum has no brothers and sisters and I don't know anything about Dad's family. Mum says that if the social services find out about her, and how little she can do...' He stopped and wiped his sleeve across his nose.

'She says they'll take her into a home and put me in one, too, because we can't manage.' The sleet had turned to rain and it hammered a drum roll on the roof of the summerhouse. Danny moved to avoid a puddle that was growing on the floor beside him.

He sniffed and took off his glasses, making a big deal of cleaning them and rubbing at them with his shirt. 'Mum would hate that. She always says we are a family and we need to stick together and help each other. She says she hates to ask me to do all this stuff, but she really needs me to be there. That's why I can't stay away from home too long. No matter what happens. I can't get in trouble with the police either. I don't know what to do, Mum's all on her own. She'll get in a terrible state if the police come to the door and I'm not there. What are we going to do?'

For once I had no idea what to say to Danny. I thought about how much I griped about having to do some chores about the house, but it was never that much, if I was honest. Mum was out a lot at the Centre and organising leaflets and things like that and even if she didn't always seem to have much time for me, she wasn't ill and she did all the house stuff and took care of dad and me, not the other way around.

Danny had to be the responsible one in his house. I thought about all the times I had been rotten to him when he rushed off home. I thought he was just being a wimp. Shows how little I knew.

That's why I sent him off. He needs to be at home so he can look after his mother. I didn't want him to be caught here with me, he's in enough trouble and the last thing he needed was to be found here with me bleeding all over the place.

I wonder how my mum will get by, with me gone, as well as Gary?

Oh God! I wish I had just gone to the police and told them the truth. Even if they hadn't really believed it, I know Ranj would have told them the truth and maybe we'd have worked something out.

Too late for that now. Too late for everything.

I was so cut up when I saw the look on Skye's face, when she realised that I'd been the one with the knife that stabbed Ranj. I wanted to wipe away the memory of that look and the way she just turned and walked away without a single word.

I keep thinking about it and seeing her face before she turned away. It won't go away no matter how much I try to put it out of my head. I never realised how much she mattered to me and how bad it would feel knowing that Skye hates me so much. It's worse because she's right. I'm rotten, through and through.

I probably deserve to die; only now I really don't want to. I want to see Skye again and I want to tell her what really happened and that I didn't mean to do it. I wish she was here now and I could tell her.

FOURTEEN: Skye

Skye left the hospital in a rage. She hated hospitals, they were places where people told you bad things, she'd always known that and today was no better. She should have avoided going to the hospital and then she would never have found out about Josh.

How could he do that to Ranj?

She always knew Josh was a bit edgy and dangerous but she had firmly believed that he was not bad, just misunderstood, and having a bad time because of his parents' obsession with his missing brother. Now she saw him in a different light. He was changing in her head, becoming ugly in every way. A person who could take a knife and plunge it into someone gentle like Ranj and worse still, to do that to someone he had once been best mates with. He tried to kill him. But why would he want to kill Ranj? That didn't make any sense.

Skye couldn't believe that the Josh she knew, and loved—if she admitted it—was some kind of cold-blooded murderer. She stopped at the corner of the street and leaned back against a doorway, unable to compete with the thoughts in her head. She let the sleet and rain fall on her face, putting her hands up to her head she squeezed them together as if trying to rid herself of the thoughts by simple pressure.

She wanted to scream at the heavens with the unfairness of it. Every time she got close to someone the world ripped them away.

The rain got heavier, and more persistent, large wet drops of water cascading from the clouds. Skye felt it soaking into her hair and clothes, until she was wet through and slowly she became aware of people looking at her strangely as they rushed for cover or put up their umbrellas.

Eventually she started to walk home, almost enjoying being so very wet, until she began to feel chilled. She felt the rain as it turned to sleet, dripping down her face, cold rivulets running down inside the collar of her t-shirt. Her jeans felt heavy with water and her canvas shoes were soggy and squelched as she walked. At least her Gran was out, at the Bingo with her friends as she was every week at this time. It meant she didn't have to face endless questions about why she was so wet or what was wrong.

She knew her Gran meant well but there were times Skye just wished she was like everyone else and had parents who gave her a hard time for being late, or lazy or soaking or anything at all, instead of the soft sad look in her Gran's eyes when she felt Skye had done something to let her down. That was much worse.

She loved her Gran; she was all Skye had, but she was so old. Her train of thought stopped there, the guilt rearing up again making her want to kick the door down rather than use the key. She stood in front of the locked door for a full five minutes contemplating some random act of vandalism before years of habit won and, slotting the key into the lock, she slipped inside.

Slamming the bedroom door shut she threw herself onto her bed, still soaking wet, and rolled into a ball, pulling a cover over herself.

She hated Josh. He had let her down. He wasn't the person she had thought he was and that hurt. Why had he done it? How could he be so hateful, so evil and cruel? How could she have loved someone like that? Did that make her a horrible person too, because she still loved him?

Eventually she fell into a deep sleep, tormented by vivid nightmares of Josh, covered in blood, attacking her with a knife as the buildings exploded all around him.

I used to think it wasn't such a big deal if someone got knifed. Everyone made such a fuss but I don't think I really considered what it would be like or what it would feel like for the person who did it, until I did it to Ranj. But even then I really felt nothing more than shock. I didn't understand or think how Ranj must have felt, I never took the time, never bothered to imagine it.

Okay, so now you know I am officially a pretty crap person, but it's true, it never touched me really, not deep down. I thought life was just something that came and went, like on the TV or films. So what if someone died. Everyone made such a big thing of it at funerals and times like that but I'd never had anyone close to me that died. I thought it was all a lot of fuss about nothing.

I never really understood it. Typical that I would only start to understand now it's too late.

It's a bit like Skye. What must it have been like for her? Everyone knew the story because she lived with her Gran, so it was the obvious question—to ask where her parents were. She never talked about it but I knew what had happened, everyone knew that her mum was killed in the gas explosion. I overheard someone saying that her Gran tried to find Skye's dad after her mother died, but no one knew who he was. Her mother had never said.

I often wondered if she remembered her mum at all but I never asked. I wish I had. Would she have told me? After the way she looked at me when she found out about Ranj I don't suppose she would ever have told me anything, She'd probably never speak to me again as long as I live.

Hmmm. That's going to be long then, is it?

Weird how we say these things and don't mean them. Things like 'As long as I live', especially when we really think that is going to be a long, long time. You don't expect it to be just a few days, or hours. Or minutes...

I really don't want to die. I want to live, to have another chance...

I never realised how important it is to know you have time. All the things you want to do or say to people.

Like my mum and dad. I want to tell them not to spend the rest of their lives looking for Gary. He doesn't want to come home. I know that. I think I've always known it. I'm not sure how or why I know. Did he tell me when I wasn't really listening and it stayed in my head as a half memory, or am I making it up? Who knows?

I want them to love me for a while, just me.

If I gave them the chance, if I had a few more hours, would I be able to get them to look at me, just me for a little, without stopping to go and look for Gary. I wouldn't mind if they looked for Gary all the time, if I could just have a bit more time to see them and speak to them both again.

Life sucks!

How stupid it that? But I wish I wasn't going to die. I wish I'd told Danny to get help. I know that's selfish but I don't really want to spend my last few minutes all alone.

It's dark.

I'm scared.

Please, somebody. I'm here.

Gary! Please, come and get me.

FIFTEEN: Summerhouse

The cold wind howled around the summerhouse, whistling eerily through all the little holes in the side. Josh and Danny sat huddled together to keep warm but it didn't make much difference.

'How long can we stay here?' Danny was shivering so much his lower lip could hardly form the words.

'Just a bit longer until it is time for the park to close.' Josh wasn't much better and his legs were feeling stiff and no matter how much he shook them out they still felt like they were seizing up. He had to move soon or he'd be in no state to run, if they had to.

'Do you think the police are still looking for us?'

'How do I know?' Josh snapped. He had been trying to think of something he could tell the police that would sound better than, 'I didn't mean to do it, officer, my hand slipped and I knifed the wrong person.' He could imagine how well that would go down.

'You'd better go home, Danny. You didn't do anything. Just tell them it was me and they'll let you go. You need to be there for your mum.'

Even as he said it Josh realised how martyrish he sounded. He couldn't help himself, he didn't really want Danny to go but felt he should at least make the offer.

Predictable as ever Danny refused to go. 'I can't just leave y-y-you, Josh.'

Josh could have applauded but at the same time he felt a niggle of guilt that he had manipulated Danny, as he always did.

'Well, we can't sit here all night. We'd better check and see if it is all quiet out there and make a run for it.'

'Where are we going, Josh?'

'You pair are going nowhere!'

Josh jumped to his feet and spun around. Harry was standing on the step, just a few paces from him.

'How did you find us?' Josh reached for his knife then realised it was no longer there. It was in the house where he had hidden it.

Harry laughed. 'Must have been the smell.' Syd and the others joined in laughing and calling Josh and Danny names.

'Heard they were after you for doing Ranj.'

'And I wonder who they heard that from?' Josh's anger bubbled up inside. 'I hadn't thought of you as a grass, Harry, but then there's probably not much lower you could get anyway. Is there? Or are you just so stupid that you think Ranj won't tell them exactly what happened?'

'I'm not the one hiding in this hell hole, waiting to do a 'midnight', am I? This looks pretty stupid to me.'

'What would you know?' Josh was trying to think

fast, to find a way out of this. He knew Harry and the rest all carried, and without a knife to defend themselves he and Danny were easy meat. This wasn't going to end well at all.

'Tell you what, Josh. Seeing as you and Danny Boy here are so clever, I'm going to give you a bit of a start. Shall we say five minutes? Then we'll come and find you.'

Josh's mind was working overtime trying to think of where they could get to in that time that would stop Harry coming after them and still keep away from the police.

He took a deep breath and tried to sound cocky. 'No problem. Don't stay up too long looking for us. Don't want you to miss your milk and cookies at bedtime.' With a sneer in Harry's direction Josh grabbed Danny's arm and took off before Harry could change his mind.

'Where...are...we...going?' wheezed Danny as they reached the edge of the park.

Josh shook his head. 'No idea yet, but we need to get as much distance between us and them as we can so I can think of somewhere.'

He led the way through the houses and through the lanes that threaded their way between the back gardens, the thundering of their footsteps matching the thrashing of his heart. It was no game, he could see in his eyes that Harry was after blood and this time it was Josh he wanted.

They skirted around the back of the takeaway

shops, keeping off the roads where the police cars did their rounds at this time of the evening.

Danny grabbed his arm. 'I can't keep going, Josh,' he panted, gasping for breath and puce in the face.

'Just a little further, Danny. We can stop in a minute or two to let you catch your breath but let's get to the flats first.'

Ahead of them were two blocks of multi-story flats. They ran into the first block and as soon as they reached the stairs Josh pushed Danny ahead of him until they got up to the first landing. Crouched down below the small window he kept a look out for Harry and the YHT while Danny slumped on the floor straining to breathe.

After a few minutes he saw that Danny was beginning to catch his breath. He was still looking scarlet with the effort of running so far but Josh knew they couldn't wait there. It was one of the worst places to be caught.

At the back of the flats was a road that only led to the rubbish dump. Josh knew the dump would be closed at this time of night and there was a reasonable amount of cover from the tall weeds and bushes used to screen it. He forced a protesting Danny to his feet.

'It's not far,' he promised him. 'We just need to get to the dump, we'll be safe there for a while, at least until it is properly dark.'

Checking the path was clear ahead they ran down the road to the dump. It was dusk and Danny stumbled over some stones on the roadway and landed flat on his face. Josh came back to help him up and they ran on again. 'Almost there,' he told him.

When they finally reached the gates Josh's heart sank. The council had been there with a strimmer and all the shelter he had hoped for was gone. He stood staring at the two inches of stubble that was all that remained of the tall weeds that had been there before.

'Shit!'

His eyes searched for an alternative place to hide and he saw a small mound where they had piled the cut vegetation.

'C'mon.' He pulled Danny towards it hoping they would be able to find somewhere to hide behind it.

There was only a little dip in the mound and behind that there was a low wall that had been hidden from view. Josh's spirits rose when he saw it. 'Perfect!' he grinned.

They went behind the wall and leaned against it gasping for breath and smiling at each other. No one would find them here. They were safe.

At least they thought so.

I feel really light, like there is nothing left of me, like I could just float away. I can't feel my arms or legs and even the snowflakes covering my eyelashes feel like they weigh three tons each. I don't even feel cold anymore. I am a feather floating away from the bird I was part of. I am caught in a breeze, fluttering...

NO! I have to stop that. I know you're not supposed to let go. I have to open my eyes, I need to stay awake otherwise when Gary comes I won't hear him.

'Gary, Gary, Gary. Gary and Katy, Gary and Katy, I saw you kissing. Hee, hee. I'm going to tell Mum.

'Ouch! Gary that hurts. Don't. Okay I won't tell. You're a nasty horrible big brother and I'm going to tell Dad you twisted my finger.

I didn't say I wouldn't tell dad, I said I wouldn't tell Mum. See!

Gary! Gary come back! Come back, Gary! I can't get up, you need to help me up. Please, Gary don't leave me alone.

Don't leave me, GARY!'

SIXTEEN: Found – and Lost

Monday evening

The last of the evening light was fading but Harry smiled as he slipped his phone into his pocket. Now that he knew exactly where to find Josh, he knew he didn't need to hurry.

'C'mon.' He strode off towards the flats with Syd and the rest following along beside him like a pack of well trained hyenas.

Harry liked that thought. He liked to think of his gang like wild dogs or hyenas. That was what they would be like when they found Josh. Harry hated Josh with all his big ideas, and smart answers but he was determined to show Josh that this was the YHT's territory. Harry wanted to show Josh that he couldn't get away with it, the YHT were hard and they were his and would do anything he wanted. He would show Josh what happened when someone crossed him, teach him not to go after Harry's girl.

What Josh didn't know was that Harry had put the word out. He had eyes all over and one of them just happened to live in the flats overlooking their hiding place. He didn't know it but there was nowhere Josh could hide that Harry wouldn't find him.

Harry took the path towards the dump, signalling to the others to keep quiet. He left two of

151

them keeping watch outside the flats and another two waited on the road. He didn't want too many witnesses, he knew how unreliable even the YHT could be, aside from Syd of course. Syd was Harry's, body and soul.

The road was tarmac so he and Syd made no noise as they approached the wall. They could hear whispering from behind it and Harry found his breath was getting more rapid as the adrenalin flowed. He loved this part of the chase, when he knew he was going to do the damage.

He was close enough now to hear them whispering. Danny was complaining about the cold, saying that it looked like it was going to snow and he wanted to go home. Harry almost gave himself away. He wanted to laugh out loud at how pathetic Danny sounded, but he stopped himself just in time.

There was a gap in the wall just beside where they were hiding, and signalling for Syd to go over the top a little further along, Harry took the last couple of steps until he was standing over the crouched figures of Josh and Danny.

'What have we here, then? Hiding, are we?'

• • •

Skye woke up shivering in her damp clothes. It wasn't that late but it was already getting dark outside. She rubbed the sleep out of her eyes and tried to make out the time on her alarm clock.

'Damn!' She got up and stripping off her damp clothes she headed for the shower and stood for a while under the pounding water until the warmth returned to her body.

'That you in the shower, Skye?'

Skye laughed. 'No, Gran it's the invisible man!'

'Want some dinner? There's some stew in the pot for you.'

She realised that her stomach was grumbling, she'd not eaten much all day and the smell of her Gran's rich meaty stew made her stomach roar again. 'I'll be down in a minute, Gran. I'm starving.'

She got dressed quickly and was soon letting Gran dole out a second helping.

'Good to see you eating it up, love,' Gran said, as if she was about two years old. But Skye just smiled. That was what her Gran was like and part of her loved it, even when she wished she wouldn't try to mollycoddle her so much.

'I've got to go out,' she said, scooping up the last of the gravy, but when her Gran's face reflected her disappointment Skye qualified it. 'Just for a little while, I won't be late.'

'Well, you be careful, Skye. You know what happened to that nice boy, Ranj.'

Like a well-aimed arrow her words hit the sorest part in her heart. 'No need to worry, Gran. I won't get into trouble.'

Slipping on her coat and grabbing a scarf at the

last minute, Skye went out. She needed to find Josh. She had to speak to him, to hear what he had to say about it. Even if he wasn't who she thought he was she didn't want to leave it like that, without asking him face to face.

She went over to his house and rang the doorbell. His mother came to the door, looking like she had been crying. 'Skye!' She looked like she wanted to drag her inside and Skye stepped back instinctively.

'Mrs Bennet?'

Josh's mother looked at her with an eager hopefulness. 'Do you know where he is?'

'Who? Josh?' she asked, knowing exactly who she meant but Skye felt she needed time to make sense of the question. 'Isn't he here?'

'No. He's run away.' The words 'just like Gary' floated in the air between them, unsaid.

'But he was at the hospital, with Danny. That's where I left them. They were talking to Ranj. His dad was waiting outside.'

As if he'd been called out, Josh's father came to the door. 'The police came to speak to him at the hospital but when we went up to the ward he was gone. They think he was the one who stabbed Ranj!' He looked a man in despair. 'Josh could never do a thing like that!'

Skye didn't know what to do or say. The last few minutes beside Ranj's bed kept running through her mind like a film on constant replay.

'You have to help us find him.' Josh's mother grabbed Skye's hand as if she would never let it go again until she promised.

'I'll go and see if I can find him, Mrs Bennet. I'm sure it will all turn out fine.'

Skye is leaning over me. I can't really see much my eyelids are too heavy, but I can feel her arms around me, hugging me. I can't move, my body is limp and I can do nothing about it. I wish...but it's too late, too late for everything. Being held close to her warmth is an amazing feeling and I want to tell her but I'm too tired.

I can hear Danny; he must have brought Skye. There's a lot of noise now, sirens I think. I don't care if the police come for me now, but Danny is babbling something and he sounds almost hysterical. He shouldn't be here. I want to tell him he should go away, before it is too late, but I can't make the words come out.

All I can focus on is Skye and her arms surrounding me, her voice calling my name. She is saying something about staying with her. Silly girl, why would I want to be anywhere else? Her blond hair is falling against my cheek. I can't feel it but I can see it through the corner of my eye.

Everything is fading. I can't feel her arms anymore.

Skye! Skye? Come back!
Don't leave me!

SEVENTEEN: Elsewhere...

It was a drab day. The streets of the city suburb were dull and dingy in the cold light and even the rain didn't seem to be able to wash away the dreariness. He trudged back to the flat avoiding the large woman standing beside the door, arguing with the landlord. It seemed that was all she ever did, but keeping his head down to avoid being noticed he slouched past and put his hand against the flaking paint, shifting his weight to give the door a good shove until it gave way.

The hallway was dark and smelled of cat pee and the stale food smell that permeated through from the dodgy café next door. At one time he would have wondered how anyone would find the food there appetising if it smelt like that, but now he knew that if you were hungry enough you'd eat anything. He knew exactly what it was like to be so hungry that you don't care what it is you're eating, as long as it is food.

He never bothered to check the mailbox, no one he knew would know where to reach him and he liked it that way. Things hadn't turned out exactly how he had imagined, but he protected his privacy. It was the thing that mattered most to him, his independence and freedom.

The top flat was the cheapest, the smallest too, but he had managed to get a room in it and he could find the rent, most weeks.

Opening the door the music hit him almost as strongly as the smell of curry. Jed was home and the only thing he could cook was curry, so the flat had a permanent smell that seemed to be ingrained in his clothes and everything he had.

'Hi Ken, how'd it go?' Jed looked up from the curry pot.

'Fine.'

'They interested?'

He shrugged. 'Sounded like they might be.'

This was the same conversation they had everyday. He almost wished he could afford to move on. He resented anyone knowing too much about him and his life, but he knew Jed didn't mean anything by it, and he owed him. Jed had said he used to be a guitarist but his hands were completely wrecked with arthritis so he couldn't play any more. They'd met at one of the first gigs he'd been to in the city.

They got talking and he soon realised that Jed knew what he was talking about. He certainly seemed to know enough about music and would pick out intricate harmonies in his old, slightly croaky voice.

Jed had offered him a room in the flat when he needed it most, and asked for a pittance of a rent. Told him he'd needed the same himself once and he was repaying the favour, and that anyway he could recognise talent when he saw it.

At first he was worried that Jed was some old perv, but as he got to know him he realised that Jed was okay. He looked much older than his 50-something years because of his crippled leg and twisted hands, but it was when Jed started talking music that he came alive and it was obvious he was a gifted musician. He'd learned lots from Jed and would probably have died of pneumonia last winter if it hadn't been for Jed giving him somewhere to stay. Even Jed's curry was occasionally a lifesaver, when he had nothing left to buy food with.

'They said they would give me a trial with them at the weekend. It'll probably come to nothing.'

'Don't put yourself down, lad. Your time will come. Don't lose faith, you've got real talent.'

'Right.' He didn't believe a word of it, so many times things had been promised and his hopes had dashed to nothing, leaving him depressed and nearly starving. But it was comforting to hear someone say it, even if it was just Jed.

'There'll be some curry left if you want it later,' Jed grinned showing his two missing front teeth, which he said had been lost in a fight, when he was working as a bouncer. It seemed like an unlikely story but so much about him was unlikely that it could just be true.

He left the grinning Jed to his curry making and he went into his room and shut the door. Picking up his guitar he started strumming a song he'd written that morning. It had been playing in his head all night and he wanted to get it down as soon as he could.

The band he'd been to see were looking for a songwriter and guitarist but he'd heard all that before and been taken to the cleaners a couple of times before he learned to protect himself; to get his money at the start and make them stick to what he had been promised. But perhaps this time it would be different. He must be about due a break.

Sometimes he wondered what was happening at home, his parents had been suffocating in their determination that he would go to university and end up working in an office every day. They'd had it all planned, all mapped out for him, all the rest of his life, but they never asked what he thought about it, and he didn't want any of it. He had his own ideas and even if it was hard at times at least he was making his own decisions, and that was what he wanted more than anything else.

He knew his parents had been trying to find him so he had changed his name and at first there were all sorts of things in the paper and even once in the news on TV. Someone told him about it, hearing his accent they wondered if it was anyone he knew but he denied all knowledge and soon moved on. It had been uncomfortably close.

He lay back on the bed and picked up the paper he'd found lying on the table in the café. He'd stopped looking at papers for anything other than work but his eye had caught on a photograph beneath the headline:

Teenage knife crime on the upsurge

The headline was followed by a load of statistics. Below it was a photograph of the victim. This was what had made him bring it back. It sent a surge of adrenaline through his veins.

He scanned it again and read the name below three or four times, almost hoping it would have changed or that he had repeatedly read it wrong.

Josh Bennett, local teenager left fighting for his life after knife attack.

He stared at the photo of a boy in school uniform, smiling for the camera. It was one of those taken by a school photographer, but the face was burned into his memory. It wasn't the face he remembered exactly, Josh had grown up a lot in the last three years. The article said he'd been stabbed and was not expected to survive.

His eyes prickled and he sniffed away the emotion in a deep breath. Josh had been a great little brother, he had been the one Gary missed most.

He screwed the paper up into a ball and threw it across the room. It was as if a door had slammed shut. It was final, there was never going to be any reason to go home now. He realised that at the back of his mind he had kept the thought that he would go back one day, just to see Josh, to explain to him why he had gone.

A few hours later he picked up the ball of news-print and tearing out the photograph he carefully smoothed it out and put it into his pocket.

EIGHTEEN: No Promises

Sunday, one month later...

Skye walked slowly up the hill, pulling her scarf closer against the cold. The early morning dawn was breaking and she was lost in thought, only just aware of the frosty sound of her feet crunching on the light covering of snow. Danny had said he would come with her if she wanted, but she didn't want any company. She had plenty to think about.

The court case would be coming up soon and she and Danny had both been called to give evidence about what happened to Josh, and Danny had to tell them about Ranj, too. She felt quite sorry for him, it was hard with his mother being so sick, but at least he didn't have to look after her all on his own now.

The police arrested all of the YHT saying that even Jack, who had phoned Harry to tell him where Josh and Danny were, was just as guilty as Harry was. Who would have thought? It gave them all a shock. The police said they were aiding and abetting, or something like that.

She hadn't slept much these last few weeks, her heart racing each time she relived that night. It had been like a nightmare.

As she ran around looking for Josh the snow had started falling and it had been getting dark. Then she ran into Danny who was in a terrible state.

She'd taken charge of things; calling the ambulance and following Danny to the spot where he had left Josh. He was lying there like an ice statue, covered in snow, with the knife still sticking out of his body. There was blood everywhere. She thought at first that she was too late; he was so pale and cold.

She could still remember how his skin felt as she cradled him in her arms and rubbed his hands to try and warm them. Little things stuck in her mind: the warm wet feeling on her knee as she knelt in his blood and felt it seeping into her jeans. How could it still be so warm when his skin felt cold and clammy?

She remembered the gentle flakes of snow as they landed on her cheeks and her own tears dropping onto his jacket leaving little clear marks, the sound of the sirens as the ambulance approached and lots of people and lights all around them. She remembered it as if it had all happened in silence, but at the back of the memory she could hear her voice sobbing his name and screaming at Josh to wake up, to stay with her, not to leave her alone again. It was as if the sound had been coming from someone else.

The path up the hill ahead of her was deserted and she was glad of that. She wanted the time to herself to think; to try and make sense of it all, although she had done little else lately. As she walked through the gates she was surprised to see someone else there, a solitary figure. It was so early in the morning she had been sure it would be deserted. It didn't look like anyone she recognised and he must have been there for a while, otherwise she would have seen him walking up the road ahead of her.

Skye hesitated, not sure she wanted to disturb him and feeling a little vulnerable up here all alone with this stranger. She watched for a while as he started moving, pacing back and forth, talking to himself. His voice carried over the grass in a low murmur, almost angry at times, but she couldn't make out a word he said. He stood still again, looking down, and fell silent. From where he was standing Skye thought he looked almost familiar.

As if her thoughts had warned him of her presence he turned and saw her. She didn't know what to do. He stared in her direction but he was too far away for her to see the expression on his face. Her feet moved almost unconsciously towards him, slowly but steadily, and he stood and watched.

Now that she was closer she realised what it was that was familiar, he reminded her of Josh, but harder and older. It took her breath away.

She stood a few feet away, her heart suddenly thundering in her chest. 'Gary?' She came closer and hesitated a moment. 'It is you, Gary, isn't it?

He looked as if he might ignore her and walk away but at the last moment he turned back to stare at the headstone.

'How...?'

'Josh talked about you, a lot. I've seen the photos he had of you.'

'Did you...?' his voice broke and he coughed. 'Did you know him well?'

'I think so, yes. I think I loved him.'

She had never said the words out loud, to anyone but they seemed right, somehow. 'He never believed you were dead, you know.'

It was maybe a weird thing to say, but Gary just nodded.

'He always said you would come back, one day. He was sure you would come back, for him.'

'I told him I would, but I thought he was sleeping.' Gary turned and looked at her. 'What's your name?'

'Skye.'

She examined his face, almost wanting it to be Josh, trying to rearrange the features in her head to make it more like him. There were similarities, his eyes especially and his expression looked a bit like Josh, but of course it wasn't him, no matter how much she wanted it to be.

'What happened? Were you there?'

Looking back later Skye thought it was the most surreal conversation she had ever had. They stood by Josh's grave as dawn broke in a clear icy sky with vibrant streaks of orange painted across it and she told Gary all about his brother's last few days. He listened quietly, soaking up the words as they tumbled from her lips.

When she had finished telling of those long minutes when she had held him in the lane as Josh slowly faded away, Gary looked up at her and gently touched her cheek to wipe away her tears. In that moment she saw Josh so clearly in his eyes.

'Will you go and see your parents?' she asked a few moments later, although she knew what his answer would be.

'There's no point, is there? I only came to say goodbye to Josh.'

'Don't you think you could just let them know you are still alive? You don't even have to say where you are.'

She thought he might be going to say yes, but he shook his head. 'What's the point? I know my mother. If I did that she would just try to find me and I don't think I could stand it, especially now. I've got nothing to say to them.'

'Could I tell them I've seen you? Give them that at least? This has been so very hard for them, first you and then losing Josh like this. Your mother never gave up on you, until Josh died. Then I think she gave up on everything. Even if I could say you were alive, it might help them a little.'

'I said, no!' He glared at her. 'Just mind your own business.'

Skye stepped back and swallowed, wishing she had kept quiet. But she had watched Josh's parents in the last few weeks and they had looked as if their whole world had faded into greyness.

She walked over and laid the flowers she had brought against the headstone. Without another word she turned and walked away. She hadn't quite reached the gates when she heard Gary running up behind her. She kept on walking, but more slowly.

'Skye! Skye, wait!'

She stopped and when she didn't turn around he stepped in front of her. She tipped up her chin and looked straight into his eyes. 'What?'

'I'm sorry. I know you were just trying to help, but you touched a bit of a raw spot there.'

She shrugged and turned her head away. 'It's your life. I shouldn't have interfered.'

'Can we at least part friends?'

Skye nodded and a smile so like Josh's flitted across his face. It made her gasp.

'I'd rather you didn't tell them I was here.'

'No probs.'

'If you wanted to give me your email, I might get in touch one day. No promises, mind.'

Skye smiled up at him. 'No promises, but I'd like that.'

'Fast-paced and
uncompromising'
The Herald

'A gritty, realistic story
with conflicted characters
that get under your skin
and prick your conscience.'
Waterstone's

'Linda Strachan is such
a compelling writer.'
Armadillo

Spider

ISBN 978-1-905537-06-8 (paperback, RRP £6.99)

A hard-hitting and provocative novel about teenage
love, loyalty and fast cars.

Spider is on his last warning. If he's caught joy-
riding again he'll be sent down, no questions asked.
He's trying to stick to the straight and narrow but
his girlfriend Deanna and mate Andy reckon he
should risk one last run.

Spider is an adrenaline-fuelled ride—a compelling
glimpse into a life spinning out of control.

•••

'A triumph of teenage fiction. The author skilfully juggles
the voices of three very different teenagers—Spider, Andy
and Deanna—in a pacy, touching story that never palls. A
compelling, insightful intertwining of credible characters.'
The Irish Examiner

'It's an intense ride. You can almost hear the wheels spin,
smell the tyres burn. Spider believes it's entirely his fault for
drawing others into his web. Strachan, however, allows the
reader to see a bigger picture of leaders and their followers.'
The Scotsman